Joyce Stranger was born in London but has always lived with animals and taken a keen interest in wildlife. She started writing at a very early age and is now the author of many bestselling novels, mainly based on her own experiences with animals; and of an equal number of children's books, one of which, *Jason*, has been filmed by Disney. She has written three books about her own dogs: *Three's A Pack*, *Two for Joy* and *A Dog in a Million*.

Joyce Stranger runs two dog clubs for pet owners and writes articles for the dog press as well as a regular column for *Cat World*. She and her husband live in Anglesey. They have three children, one an electronics engineer, one a vet and one a zoologist; and they have six grandchildren and four step-grandchildren.

Also by Joyce Stranger

CHIA THE WILDCAT
A DOG CALLED GELERT
A DOG IN A MILLION
THE JANUARY QUEEN
KHAZAN
LAKELAND VET
NEVER COUNT APPLES
NEVER TELL A SECRET
ONE FOR SORROW
THE RUNNING FOXES
TWO'S COMPANY
WALK A LONELY ROAD

and published by Corgi Books

Joyce Stranger

The Hound Of Darkness

CORGI BOOKS

*Dedicated to Catherine Williams who has given me the
pleasure of having a ready-made grand-daughter,
old enough to be thinking already of her own
future career. With my love.*

THE HOUND OF DARKNESS
A CORGI BOOK 0 552 13287 X

Originally published in Great Britain by
J. M. Dent & Sons Ltd.

PRINTING HISTORY
J. M. Dent & Sons edition published 1983
Corgi edition published 1987

This book is set in 10/11pt Times

Corgi Books are published by Transworld Publishers
Ltd., 61–63 Uxbridge Road, Ealing, London W5 5SA, in
Australia by Transworld Publishers (Aust.) Pty. Ltd.,
15–23 Helles Avenue, Moorebank, NSW 2170, and in New
Zealand by Transworld Publishers (N.Z.) Ltd., Cnr. Moselle
and Waipareira Avenues, Henderson, Auckland.

Printed and bound in Great Britain by
Cox & Wyman Ltd., Reading, Berks.

At Builth Wells, Brecon, there is a cairn on the mountain. The mountain is named Cefn Carn Cafell. On top of the cairn is a stone which has a paw mark embedded in it. This is supposed to be the paw of King Arthur's dog, Cafell. Arthur built a cairn and topped it with this stone. Legend has it that if someone moves the stone, it always returns to its place.

Myddfai, in Carmarthenshire, is the magical place of Wales. Here, long ago, a fairy came out of Llyn Fan Fach, the lake five miles to the south of the town. A local man fell in love with her and courted her. In the end she agreed to marry him, and brought with her a herd of sheep, cattle, goats and horses. They lived happily at a farm called Esgair Llaethdy just outside the town, and the fairy had three sons.

The farmer had been told he must never strike her, but one day he saw her daydreaming, and tapped her gently to make her look at him. She stayed, but told him he had only two more chances. One day she cried, as people will, at a wedding, and to cheer her up, he patted her on the shoulder; that was the second time. Many years later, she laughed at a funeral, glad that the suffering of the newly dead person was over; her husband tapped her, telling her she should not think like this. That was the third time, and she took all her beasts and returned to the lake.

She never saw her husband after that, but she used to come up from the lake and teach her sons about herbal medicine; her descendants are still famous for their knowledge of herbal lore.

There are stories of will-o'-the wisps all over the British Isles; some are airy lights misleading people, others are the ghosts of animals. One such story, whose origin cannot be traced, was told to me by an old man in a Sussex village. This is a story of a dog that lost his master through death, because he would not follow the dog to safety in darkness and mist. The dog returns whenever a traveller is lost and those who follow him are always safe. Those who ignore him fall over the cliffs and die, as his master died.

There are more legends about Arab horses than about any other breed in the world; the legends are worldwide because the horses were so coveted that they were bought in every country where horses were bred to improve the local breeding.

The Koran is filled with commands to take care of the horse, which was vital to the existence of Mohammed's people.

Some of the Arab horses have a mark known as the Prophet's Thumbmark; it is near the crest on the animal's neck, and the hair grows from a central point, lying flattened as if a thumb had been pressed into it.

CHAPTER ONE

THEY called the mountain the Old Man.

Long ago, when the human race was very young, men worshipped him; men placated him; men sang songs to him, and built great fires of sacrifice on his slopes.

Now, they still feared him. He was not the highest of the mountains round them, but he was the fiercest.

He towered above the village. In winter, snow came down to the tree line and below; snow that sometimes threatened them by avalanche; snow that sometimes buried sheep and buried climbers; snow that melted and turned the rivers into raging torrents, and transformed the waterfall into a fierce and savage creature that tore its way through the trees and spilled over the streets, that flooded the houses and drowned the chickens, and the dogs and the cats, the sheep and the cattle, as well as the horses, and sometimes even men.

From the end cottages it was possible to see the wicked slopes of the Devil's Kitchen; beyond was the Cauldron that was, they said, beloved by witches.

No one believed in witches, white or black, any more, but for all that, if the cattle sickened or a child was ill, they went to Angharad, who was the nearest creature to an angel that anyone in the village had ever seen.

Her hands soothed headaches away; her gentle voice and wisdom helped those who grieved; she came when neighbours quarrelled, or when a baby was born, or an old man or woman died; no one could imagine life without her.

They called her the Wise One; she alone loved the Old Man. She loved him in summer when his slopes were bright with heather; she loved him in winter when snow hid gully and crevice and covered his rutted flanks.

A death for the Old Man: a yearly sacrifice, they said in the village, and tried to stop the local lads climbing. They watched climbers pass through, rucksacks on their backs, eagerness in their eyes, and hoped they would all return safely.

Every year, the Mountain Rescue Land Rover drove often up the pass; every year the dogs went searching. Every year, the Old Man claimed a victim — sometimes more than one.

There was the little slope — such a little slope that the Rescue men called it Nameless; beyond it was the Valley of Fear. Here, when the wind grew strong and roared down the slopes, when snow filled the gullies, and the passes were closed, and far below cars slithered and slid, and drivers' hearts beat wildly with every gentle caress of the brake, death lurked for anyone that came.

Angharad lived at the foot of the slope, where the fields came down to the cold waters of the lake that, legend said, hid the lady and her cattle — the lady that had come from the lake long ago and married a mortal. Merfyn, who had married her, had been left with his baby son, and no wife to rear the boy.

His descendants were in the village still, so people said — children that were half fairy; and certainly where the village children were dark, these children were tall and fair, with brilliant blue eyes that seemed to search into a man's soul.

They loved the water and were excellent swimmers, outdistancing every other child. There were always two or three in each generation. Angharad had been one of them, but her blond hair was now white. She was old, though did not look as old as her years; no one in the village could remember when Angharad had been

8

born, or even if she had ever married. She stayed with them, it seemed for ever, ageless, her eyes as bright as those of a younger woman. And often she walked beside the lake and picked the wild flowers, binding them into garlands to place on the Gipsy's grave.

No one knew who the Gipsy had been or when he had lived. The grave had been there for ever, a tiny, tumbled cairn of stones, bright with flowers that the gipsy people laid when they passed by; bright with flowers that Angharad put there, flowers for memory. Memory was what made man rise above the animals, she said often to the children who helped her with the garlands. Memory, and pity, and the power to pass on experience — to teach others.

She did not teach in school but there were always children in her cottage — learning to sew and bake, learning to count, to read, to write, and to tend her small garden and help her with the herbs she grew.

She taught the children to swim in the shallows of the lake; it could save them from death when the Old Man flooded the village. She taught them to watch the clouds, to know when thick mist would hide the foot-slopes and make them dangerous; to know when the giant thunder clouds towered above the Old Man's head, and lightning raged on the rocks, and when it was wise to take shelter (but never under a tree or near a tall post).

She taught the children to read the sky; to know north from south and east from west, and where the village lay, from every direction, so that they could follow the landmarks if they were lost. She took them and showed them the dangers of the footslopes, the need to watch every step, the bogs that no man had ever plumbed where cattle and horses — and maybe men, too, lay buried for ever; the treacherous green mosses that betrayed the wetlands; the gullies in the ground.

She gathered rosehips and made syrups which she gave to mothers for their babies; she made wine from

9

elderberries; and blackcurrant syrups that, sweetened well with honey, soothed sore throats.

She made cough syrups from coltsfoot and pine and honey; she kept bees in her tiny orchard, and told them all the village news. It was never wise to forget to tell the bees. They knew of birth and of death; of weddings and of the triumphs of the children and the grown-ups; they knew when Angharad was happy: she sang to them when she was sad.

She sang often. Angharad coached two choirs; the singing of the valley was famous.

In summer the children sat in her little front garden and listened to her stories of the old days; of witch women and wise women; the stories of Merlin the magician, and of Arthur — the greatest king of all. They knew that the pawmark of a dog, high on the hill above them, was the pawmark of Arthur's great hound Cafell — a hound that had outrun the north wind and the snow that came howling out of the sky one winter night, threatening the village.

That had been long ago. The great dog had raced, his coat snow-rimed, and barked to warn everyone. The cottages at the foot of the Old Man were emptied, and when the avalanche crashed down on them nobody was hurt.

Angharad spoke as if Arthur and Merlin were alive still and were friends of hers, gone on their travels, but friends who would come again. When the wind howled at night when she was sitting with one child or another whose parents were visiting friends, she would hush them saying, 'It is only Cafell crying on the wind to tell us he is on guard and no harm will come to us.' The children learned to love the wind and the crying sound of the great hound which had protected the king in his time and which still protected them, casting his spell around the village, so that it seemed a better place to live than most.

Villagers who were caught on the mountains often told of a great hound that appeared to them, half hidden in mist, which led them safely down the slopes before vanishing. He was larger than any mortal dog, but no one feared him. If Cafell were hunting then everyone was safe.

Sometimes climbers came to the village and stayed in the homes of the children. They heard the stories of Cafell and laughed at them among themselves. One dark night, when no sane man would have braved the peril of the slopes, a young student set out alone to climb the big buttress by moonlight, at the end of the place the Rescue men called Nameless.

It was a dark night, and, as the moon lifted above the peaks, light glinted on snow. Out of the darkness came a great dog which herded the man backwards, down the slope and down the hill, towards the village, cutting him off from the pass.

Towards three in the morning the mountain rumbled, and great rocks fell from the top towards the steep cliff that the young man had wanted to climb. He was sitting on the rocks near the village street, watching the hound which sat in the shadows, but moved, snarling, whenever he moved.

The sound of the thundering rocks died away. The moon rose high and clear, and the shadows were empty. There was no sign of a dog.

Angharad came to meet him as he returned to the village street.

'Did you climb?' she asked.

He shook his head.

'There was a great hound that wouldn't let me pass; he snarled and bayed and cut me off from the slope, and I couldn't go forward.'

'That was Cafell,' Angharad said, and the man, who was a stranger to the village, never even knew that he had been herded by Arthur's hound, dead for many centuries, but which still kept men from death whenever he could.

'There are always new legends being born,' Angharad told the children one autumn day when a chill wind

11

heralded winter. 'They come from the past and they come from the present. One day you may be part of them; any one of us, remembered, in time to come, for a deed well done, will perhaps provide a "Once Upon a Time" story for those yet to be born, helping to guard them from danger. Those who can see are safe; those who deny life itself, will never prosper.'

The children called in on their way home from school, drawn as always by the scent of new-baked bread; by the teasing smell of the herbs Angharad was drying; by the knowledge that there would be home-made biscuits and lemon drinks for them.

They were greeted at the door by the two marmalade cats, Topsy and Polly, who were more mischievous than any monkeys could be, and yet had learned to leave alone the birds that came for suet and for nuts. There were always birds in the bushes in Angharad's garden. She whistled to them and they answered.

She loved to watch the wild birds gather on the lake; to see the lark soaring in the sky; to listen to the night owl as he called his lonely note across her garden, or perched on her gatepost, his head turning to look for movement in the grass; to hear the curlews trilling softly in the water meadow beyond her garden.

The village dogs lay at Angharad's gate but rarely came in because Cafell visited her garden. They knew him and they saw him, and they respected him; yet they were aware that he left no pawmark and had no smell.

The children felt that the village sheltered them from the world. But Angharad knew that the world would come to the village; that it would provide refuge for others, as it always had. Refugees had come in the past. The family who now lived in the mill had come from Spain, but so long ago that everyone forgot they did not belong here; their names were now village names, and only their dark skin and blue-black hair and deep, dark eyes betrayed their origins.

The family in the Smithy, which had long forgotten horses, came from Jersey, having fled when the

Germans overran the islands. They had started a bakery and baked the best bread in that part of the country. People came for miles to buy.

There was history in the village, and legend — all mixed up. The big Druid stone in the school-yard still frightened the children. It reared towards the sky, its bent tip pointing directly at the top-most peak on the Old Man, and they sang songs to it when they played outside, never knowing why.

The song they sang had been sung in the village for as long as anyone, even Angharad, could remember.

'Standing stone, standing stone,
Here at midnight I come alone;
Flowers I bring, and a song I sing,
That you to the village good luck may bring.'

They all sang it, or whispered it as they passed, holding out two fingers to keep the devil away, though none of them knew that that was what the sign meant. Their parents had done it, and their parents before them.

Listening to Angharad telling of the days before they had been born, before the days of motor cars, when every man rode or drove a horse, they tried to imagine the village as it had been then.

'It has changed little,' Angharad said. She lifted Topsy and held her close, and the big cat purred, a deep, throbbing, happy note that hummed on the air. Polly came jealously and was lifted, too.

'Legends are made all the time. Even now, someone is coming to the village who will make a new legend for us; a legend of horses.'

No one in the village had horses. The children looked at her, surprised. She smiled back at them.

'How do you know?' asked a small girl named Emily, her dark hair tied back with a scarlet ribbon, brown eyes wondering.

13

Angharad lifted her tea cup, and showed them the pattern in the leaves.

'It could be a dragon,' said one of the boys.

'It is a horse,' Angharad said. 'We can't breed dragons now.'

'Did anyone ever breed dragons?' asked Emily.

'Who knows?' Angharad said, and laughing, sent the children home. Indoors, she went to the window and looked up at the Old Man.

'Be kind to us this winter,' she said.

There was so much power in him; in his rocks and his clouds, in the thunder that rumbled on his peaks and the wild shafts of lightning that could kill man or beast. Two cows had died in the meadow only that summer; and a tree lay, ripped in two, making a bridge across the river. There was power in the rocks; and power in the wind; and power in the water that flooded out of the darkness.

There was death on his slopes.

She could never forget him; he had her deepest respect. It was wise, always, to remember that he could often be treacherous, yet that made no difference to her feelings for him.

Tonight the wind was rising. Rain beat suddenly against the window.

Somewhere out on the slopes the wind howled like a dog.

'Guard us, Cafell,' Angharad said, and drew the curtains against the dark, isolating herself with the bright flames of the coal fire, the purring cats, and the white cloth spread for her supper.

The wind whimpered, like a dog shut out in the rain, and hoofbeats rang out along the village street. Angharad lifted the curtain. The orange street lights shone on two of the most beautiful horses she had ever seen. A mare, and a stallion such as Arthur would have been proud to ride. They were led by a dark, bearded man who turned towards her briefly, not seeing her. She thought his eyes were the saddest

14

eyes imaginable. The stallion nudged him, rubbing his head against his master's arm. The man turned to him, eyes suddenly blazing with pride.

'It has begun,' Angharad said to the leaping flames, and the two cats deafened the air with their purrs.

CHAPTER TWO

LEGENDS are built slowly.

The man and the horses had been part of the village, and yet not part, for almost a year, when the letter came.

The letter lay on the mat. The man looked down at it. He had been waiting for a long time. He had been hoping for a long time.

The last words he had heard, as the ship that was to take him into exile drew away from the pier were, 'Your son will come to you when it is safe.' He stood on the deck till the land vanished, looking hungrily at scenes that he would never see again.

Such a small object; a letter. A pale blue envelope, edged with bright colours. The thin, spidery, foreign handwriting; the unfamiliar name that he now used; the stamp of the country in which he had been born. Once his head had graced those stamps.

Now another man's head looked at him, from eyes that he had once thought friendly; treacherous eyes, and a treacherous lying tongue. A hand that had offered friendship, and yet had signalled to the quick, stuttering guns to fire upon him and his family, his friends and his men. His cousin's eyes.

The envelope roused memories. The name of the stranger with the horses was Raoul — a name near enough to the name that had once been his. Few men used it, in friendship or in enmity. He had come to a lonely place.

Once he had commanded armies; had owned aeroplanes; had boasted a host of friends. He had gone to an English school, long ago. He had had a wife, in the

16

western style who had borne him a son. He had married late and the boy was trebly dear to him.

Kneeling by his wife's side, he had seen bright blood staining her white robes. He stayed until she died. Then Ali seized him by the arm and pulled him unceremoniously through the backquarters of his home, out into the night, where the saddled horses waited. Only two horses: the pride of his stud — his noble stallion Mahruss, and his much loved little mare, Djeroua, who was as brave as Mahruss and who would run till the winds of the world were left behind her.

'You must live,' his friends said. 'One day, you will return.'

Raoul knew he would never return. His world was gone and a new world had come, a world he did not like or understand. Young men had brave ideas; young men had new aims; young men used bombs and torture and guns. He was old now and had never used such methods. He could never go back.

He ached for his own land; for the desert sands and the bright stars in the deep, dark sky at night; for a moon more luminous than the moon in this country; for a sun that baked down, warming a man. Here, he was always cold.

He had come to England, and then to Wales, with two horses, both beyond price; with five emeralds from his father's hoard, stitched carefully into his clothes. He had landed, a stranger in a strange land, in a wintry world that he had forgotten existed. Frost rimed the grass and he could see no further than the end of the grey streets.

People passed him, turning away their heads. He was alien to them; perhaps a threat to them. He didn't know. He only knew he longed for his child to come to him; he longed to swing the boy into his arm, to hold him close, to teach him to love horses, and to breed horses, as his father had bred them, for here in this new land was his future, and it was the only future he knew.

No one knew he had once been a king; even though his was only a tiny kingdom at the other side of the world. He had not wished to rule.

'Why must I?' he had asked his father, and his father, who had been an old man, having married late, too, had told him that he was born to rule — and so it was willed. He had no choice.

He was tired of court routine; of men he dared not trust; of friends who might be false; and had lavished his affection on his cousin, the son of his father's younger brother. He had trusted him with his life; and had almost lost it as a result.

Men he could trust had taken his son two days before the firing began, as his spies brought news. He did not know, then, who lay behind the rebellion; who had ordered the guns; who had chosen to betray him. He only knew when his cousin came running and fired the shots that killed his wife; one shot hit him in the arm. He had not been meant to escape.

The knowledge was still bitter, and he trusted no one. He could not make friends, even here, as he feared false tongues. He did not want anyone to know of his past. He was an alien in a foreign land; a simple man, living as the village people lived, in a house that was larger than most because he needed stables for his horses. He also needed land for them to graze, and small houses did not have either.

He lived alone, with Annyl from the village coming in daily to clean the house and prepare his food. She arrived at ten and she left at three; in the evening he heated his own supper, enjoying the chore.

He, too, lived in the shadow of the Old Man, but the village lay between them.

Spending the day with his horses, he chose to forget the desperate months of hunting for a home; the travelling round the country; the stables in which he had had to leave his stallion and his mare, never sure if they would be treated as he would treat them. Once they had been his pride; now they were his life.

He had come upon his new home by chance, talking to a groom in a brewery stable, where the big shires dwarfed his elegant animals. Thomas had been Welsh and hated the city where he worked; but he had to work among horses, and there was no work in his own village. Raoul was tempted to offer him a job, but that would not have been wise. Thomas had his own life — a wife and two small sons, Rhys and Dafydd.

'There is a house for sale in my father's village,' he said. 'It has land and stables, but it needs a great deal spent upon it. It has been empty for several years.'

Raoul had boarded a train that day, and had driven by taxi to the village. The house was old and in need of paint. It stood, gaunt and lonely, on a bare hillside, but the fields were lush with grass; and the old stables were sound and in excellent repair.

'They bred horses here, long ago,' the taxi driver said.

Raoul sold his jewels. They had been flawless, and brought him enough to live on for the rest of his life, though he would need to sell horses, too.

He bought another mare; not as beautiful as Djeroua, but very lovely. Mahruss guarded them both. Raoul bought a book on the history of his lovely Arab breed, and was intrigued to find that even in England, long ago, the Arabians had been famed beyond all other horses. He knew they had been precious but had had no idea they were worth fortunes — immense fortunes — more than anything paid for them now.

King Edgar, in the tenth century, had held a race at his court where two Arabian horses had run against one another: a stallion named Arundel, and a mare named Truncefice. The stallion won, but the mare was remembered, too, in history, and Raoul named his second mare after her.

If she had a male foal, Raoul would name him Arundel; it had been a famous name. Two centuries later a knight named Sir Alured de Vere had sold another stallion called Arundel to King Richard for £25,000; a sum in the twelfth century that was beyond computation now.

Once he had raced his own horses. Memory hurt.

His horses would never again match themselves against the desert winds. They would never again bear him proudly among his own people. He looked out of the window, at the stallion in his stable, head looking towards the house, longing for his master. Soon they would work together, and the horse would show his paces. Perhaps one day Roaul would compete in dressage events; as yet, he did not want to go out among his fellow men. He had lived here only a few months; wary months, lonely months, in a land where two languages were spoken daily and neither of them was his.

His tongue had almost forgotten the words of his own country, though he used them when grooming the horses.

He had written on a parchment a saying of his own folk in his own language. It was framed above the mantelpiece in the room where he kept his records. It was familiar, well loved, and helped to make a new home.

'After man, the most eminent creature is the horse; the best employment that of rearing it; the most delightful posture that of sitting on its back; the most meritorious of domestic actions that of feeding it.'

Mohammed himself had said that as many grains of barley as are contained in the food we give a horse, so are the many indulgences we daily gain by giving it.

Raoul was earning himself a sure place in Heaven for no one but he ever tended his beauties. They were far too precious to trust to unskilled lads, and he did not encourage girls. Women did not show their faces in public places in his own land. He could not, even now, get used to women who worked and walked and rode as men, and who seemed to him far from being feminine.

20

He longed for his wife. He did not even know where they had buried her. He had changed the laws of his land so that each man had only one wife. But his cousin had changed them again.

The letter was still in his hand, unopened. He was afraid of the news it carried.

He needed his son. The boy would be twelve years old now; it was time for him to learn how to breed horses; there would be no other life for him in this new world of the 'eighties.

Raoul slit the top of the envelope neatly, using a silver-handled paper knife. It reminded him of home. He had bought it in an antique shop in the nearby town several weeks before.

The words leaped at him.

'The boy is dead. He died of an illness of which many chidren have died. We send you greetings, and we sorrow for the past. We hope all is well with you in your new home.'

Raoul tore the letter into fragments, and burned them in the fireplace. Outside the window the wind whipped through the stable yard, throwing straws before it. There was always wind on the hill. He heard it moaning, and when the wind moaned his dog Naseem howled as if he were answering another dog.

The sea was not far away; two miles as the seagulls flew. The gales that whipped the sea to frenzy tore at his home. Rain drummed often on the windows. The fields below were marshy, but here the land was drained. He was fortunate. He had chosen well, knowing what he needed.

The stallion whinnied, and the big dog that lay at the door, watching his master, barked twice. Naseem was a German Shepherd, a big handsome dog, as regal as the stallion. Mahruss loved the dog; they often raced against one another, and when the stallion was

21

being trained, the dog lay watching, as if aware of every mistake.

The dog barked again. Raoul went out into the yard.

The dirtiest lad he had ever seen stood looking at the horses. His clothes were torn; his hair unkempt, lying long and greasy on his shoulders. But his eyes, which were large and dark, were staring at the mares with an expression that Raoul had not seen for a long time.

'They're terrific,' the boy said.

'Yes,' Raoul agreed. 'Who are you?'

'Micky. I'm an Irish gipsy; born with horses, bred with horses. I want a job. I haven't had a job for two years; no one wants a gipsy.' He grinned, showing teeth that were startlingly white in his dirty face. 'I need some place to live; a room above the stable would do. I know horses, mister. Honest I do.'

'Then why will no one employ you?'

'No money, most of 'em. And they don't trust gipsies. You know what they say. "If there's a law they break it; whatever they find, they take it, so never you talk to a gipsy or look in a gipsy's eye." ' He grinned again. 'You can trust me around horses. Me grandad was a whisperer.'

'A whisperer?'

'He whispered to 'em and they followed.'

'You grew up in Ireland?' Raoul asked, intrigued in spite of misgivings.

'In Liverpool; me mum was one of the People. Me dad was an Irish sailor. Her folk didn't like him one bit, so she left them. We lived in a house, but I didn't like it. No horses, so mostly I went with me grandad. When he died, I left home for good; been living rough and doing what I could since then. But it's horses I need; they're in me blood. Watch.'

He walked over to the stallion and breathed softly into his nostrils. Raoul watched. Mahruss did not like strangers and when he was free, would rear on his

22

hind legs and paw the air, threatening them, warning them to keep away from him. If they disobeyed him, he kicked.

Raoul was curious. He opened the stable door and Mahruss walked out, every muscle aware of its own power. He walked to his master and rubbed his head down his shirt. It was his greeting gesture, always. He reared above the man, and settled his hooves on his shoulders, almost sitting, gazing into his master's eyes. Raoul rubbed the soft muzzle very gently; it was dark and velvet smooth. Wise eyes looked into the man's face.

Micky moved, and the stallion stood, pawing the ground.

'You beauty,' Micky whispered. 'You beauty.'

The horse moved towards the boy.

He dipped his head and stood, quite still, allowing the dirty fingers to stroke behind his ear. He leaned his head against the boy's caressing hand.

Raoul went into the tack room and came out again with his saddle.

'Saddle him,' he said.

This would be the test. Mahruss was very particular about his saddle; it had to be placed gently, tightened surely, every movement skilled. He did not like strangers handling him at all.

The saddle was on; it looked like a conjuring trick.

There was not a sound from Mahruss. He waited for Raoul to mount.

It was not time for training, but the man rode his horse around the yard. He watched the Irish boy's face.

'You can stay,' Raoul said, as he dismounted. 'For a month. We'll see after that. You have to work, all the time; not just with the horses. The pasture must be kept free of ragwort in summer; weeds need to be cut away; the stables need cleaning; there is much to do.'

'Give me clothes and food, and a little money and I'm yours,' Micky said. 'And a bath; I don't look like this all the time; been living rough.'

'How old are you?' Raoul asked.

'Nineteen. I'm small, weedy. People think I'm only fourteen. Me mum was small and me dad would've only come up to your shoulder. I can work. Honest.'

'We will see.'

It was lonely here, and the boy was young and lively and chattered happily. Raoul could teach the lad about Arab horses. He did not seem to notice that Raoul was a foreigner; Micky treated him as he would have treated any man, on a basis of equality that took for granted that Micky himself was as good as anyone. He had a cocky grin, and an endearing manner.

'There's a cottage behind the stable. If you can clean it up and renovate it you can have it for your own while you're here,' Raoul said. He led the way across the yard, Mahruss following, the dog behind him. Micky saw a tack room, neatly kept; a barn filled with hay; a stack of piled straw, covered by a tarpaulin. Beyond the stack was the old cottage. Inside was rubble — work enough for ten men, but he had never had a place of his own. He had been living wild for almost a year and he was tired of roaming and being hungry and cold. He belonged with horses and these horses were such that he would sell his soul to care for them.

Their master was a bit strange, but they'd get on. Anyone who could keep horses in this condition was a man after Micky's own heart.

Micky stood, looking at the mares. Djeroua was in foal. He had never seen any mare like her. He thought of the foal being born; he remembered standing in his grandfather's field, watching the foals run at dusk, kicking up their heels, delighted to be alive.

'There's nothing like them,' he said, not intending to speak the words aloud.

'In my country, the man who breeds horses is above all other men,' Raoul said. 'Come, I will lend you clothes, and tomorrow you must buy yourself something decent to wear.'

'Have you always lived in this country?' Micky asked.

'I went to school in England, long ago,' Raoul said. 'But now I've decided to live in Wales.'

Micky nodded. It explained a lot, and he had no further curiosity.

Later that night, bathed and shaved, his hair clean and neatly brushed, he proved to be a good-looking boy. Dressed in Raoul's slacks and a yellow shirt, although they were far too big, his skin darkened by sun and wind to a shade that almost matched Raoul's, Micky felt revived.

He ate as if he had not seen food for months. And after eating, he took the dishes and washed up, without needing instruction. Later, bedding the horses, he whistled as he worked, spreading the straw under them thickly. He fondled the younger mare and she rubbed her head against him.

'When will the foal come?'

'In March,' Raoul said. 'It was not intended; Mahruss jumped the fences. It will be a good foal; but I would have waited a year. Trunca is newly in foal, too.'

'It's an odd name,' Micky said, as he shot the bolts on the door, and watched Raoul fix the padlocks for the night.

'She's named after a famous mare that once raced at a Royal Court, nearly a thousand years ago,' Raoul said. 'Truncefice. I named her for luck and for speed; and for good foals from her.'

Mahruss was waiting for them, a last faint sunbeam gilding his coat. He stood, outlined against the sky, as if he were posing, perhaps for a photograph, perhaps for a statue that would immortalize him for centuries to come.

He moved proudly, arrogantly, a king among stallions, and well aware of the fact.

Micky was watching him, and Raoul watched Micky, knowing that here was a lad in a million; there was no mistaking the expression in his eyes. To Micky the horse was king of all the beasts.

Raoul smiled. It was good to have someone to talk to. He had not realized how lonely he was, isolated here with his horses, and only a village girl who helped in the house who was too afraid of him to speak.

'Will I do?' Micky asked, standing at the foot of the stairs before turning towards the little room that had been prepared for him beyond the kitchen. Most of the rooms in this barn of a house seemed to lack furniture of any kind.

'I think you will do,' Raoul said, He could not be sure on so little knowledge. 'We try for a month, yes?'

Micky nodded, and closed the door behind him. It was good enough.

That night Angharad laid a fresh garland on the Gipsy's grave.

CHAPTER THREE

MICKY woke early and was out before light shone from the sky. The moon was a ghost of herself, a thin segment, hanging above the starkly outlined hills, which gleamed with snow. The Old Man's slopes were deeply hidden.

Micky could not start work on the horses. He had forgotten about the padlocks. Raoul was a careful man. His horses were his only wealth, his only possessions. They were his friends, his family — his link with the past.

On the back of his stallion he was a king again, king in his own small kingdom. But it was no longer a realm with subjects of his own. His kingdom was a house and four fields, a drive, and a tangle of garden. It was a strange home in a strange land where he himself was a stranger, but it was his.

It was all that was left to him. Riding Mahruss down the deserted lanes, he thought about his wife and son who he would never see again.

Could a man help being born as he had been born, son to a man who was king? He had not asked for life; it had come to him. His son had never wished to be king either.

When he rode, thoughts fought in his mind. There was not one man or woman here to whom he could talk easily, in friendship. No one spoke his own tongue, and it was hard to phrase words in a language he had learned so long ago.

Raoul, waking, saw Micky standing in the yard, looking at the mountains. He dressed, and joined the boy.

'I want to make sure he's real,' Micky said, and Raoul, looking down at the Irish gipsy lad, knew that here at least was someone who loved horses with all his mind.

He opened the door, and Mahruss came to greet them. Micky looked up at the glorious head and his heart lurched as he fell passionately in love. His grandfather would have given life itself for a horse like this — a stallion beyond price.

He looked at him, remembering the standard for the Arabian; his grandfather had worshipped the breed, but never in his life could he aspire to owning a horse like this.

Short head, and great refinement. It was there in this aristocrat — this prince, this emperor among stallions. In every curve, in every bone, in the swell of the cheek, in the softness of the lips, in the magnificent, brilliant eyes. Micky reached towards the horse, and Mahruss dipped his head, and bent downwards, so that he breathed softly into Micky's cupped hands; a superb muzzle, and small — small, but perfect.

A muzzle softer than velvet, gentle, warm, with nostrils that suddenly widened in excitement, as Raoul moved behind the gipsy. Mahruss whinnied a delighted whicker of joy to see his master so early in the day.

The moon had slipped from the sky. Light was shadowing the far hills. The first glow of the sun turned the snow the colour of flamingos. Raoul looked about him; at the cobbled yard, mysterious in the early light, at the glitter in Micky's eyes as he fondled the horse; this was his only future.

'Can I bring him out?'

Raoul nodded, and watched deft hands slip on the halter, watched the horse step out proudly, his neck arched, his eyes gleaming. Mahruss spoke with his eyes; he spoke gently to his mares, admiring them, coaxing them; he spoke to Raoul, and now he was challenging Micky, who grinned at him and patted the beautifully curved neck, pulled gently at the shining

28

mane, and told the horse in his own way that no nonsense would be allowed.

'My grandad had a stallion once; a rare brute,' Micky said. 'Nothing like this.'

He devoured the horse with his eyes, savouring every inch of him; such a horse — everything about him perfect; every curve of his body splendid, every movement controlled and eager.

Raoul watched as Micky led the stallion to the field.

Opening the gate he led the horse to the grass. Mahruss stood on his hind legs, pawing the air, and bucked high. He whickered, greeting the day, and the mares answered him. He began to run, up the slope of the field and down the far side, kicking up his hind legs like a young colt, delighted to be free after being shut in all night.

There was a glitter of frost on the grass, but the ground was still soft. Mahruss cantered, and then eased into a fast trot, covering the ground smoothly — floating over the ground.

'He's beautiful,' Micky said, awe in his voice, unable to take his eyes off the animal.

'Someone writing about the Arabian horse, many years ago said that nature, when making the Arab, made no mistake. He was right . . . everything about him is perfect.' Raoul never tired of watching Mahruss. When the work was done, he stood at the gate, watching the stallion exercise himself; watching him rear against the sky, pawing the air, and buck, and run proudly, his head always held in that wonderful arch, always aware that he was regal, a king among horses, none excelling him.

'There's work to do,' Raoul said, and reluctantly Micky came to the stables. The mares were taken out and the day's tasks begun.

The bedding had to be removed and carted to the midden; the floors cleaned; food given to each of the three; water buckets filled and allowed to stand, to take the chill off them; a film of ice broken on the trough in the yard and hot water added; loose straw swept, and the yard cleaned and tidied.

Each mare had to be groomed. Micky was given Trunca, and Raoul groomed his other mare — his beauty — soon to foal. Djeroua, as always, leaned her head against him, savouring every moment of her brushing. Her silky mane was combed until it gleamed; her tail matched it for elegance. Her soft, dark eyes watched Micky, inspecting him, as if she wondered about him, and was not yet sure whether she could trust him. She was lighter in colour than Trunca, though not so dark as Mahruss. The bulge of the foal showed, and Micky longed for the birth.

He had wandered for so long; working where he could, but never with horses. He had not touched a horse, except to pet it, since his grandfather died; and that was four years before. He had lived nearly all the time with his grandfather, always around the stables, listening to the men. His grandfather's life had revolved around horses.

There had never been time for Micky to learn well. But he had handled all sorts from the ugly, ungainly, bad-tempered hack that had tossed Micky into the depths of the midden, to the little elegant mare that had fetched a top price at an auction. Grandfather had been a middle-man; buying them and selling them.

A good few tricks, too, Micky had learned in his time, but no tricks were needed here. No need to change the shape of a mane to hide a bad head; no need to add lustre to these gleaming coats; no need to try and sell either of the mares for virtues that did not exist, because both had every virtue. Almost.

Trunca, sensing that Micky had begun to dream, pulled his hair with her teeth.

He spoke sharply and she reared. He quieted her.

'I forgot to warn you,' Raoul said, a smile on his face. His mouth was half-hidden in his dense, grey-streaked beard. 'She does not allow your thoughts to wander, that one.'

30

Micky laughed and returned to his work, concentrating.

Trunca, once she was groomed, was put in the far field. Raoul took Djeroua, and led her gently down the lane, to exercise her, before putting the two mares together. It would soon be time to train Mahruss.

Micky was left to prepare the feeds; detailed weights of each of the ingredients were written down for him. Grandfather had never fed horses this way. Hay in the nets; nuts in the bags, and that was it, though he had often spoken to Micky of his young days, and of his own recipes for feeding an in-foal mare to get the best foal possible from her.

Oats and bran; vegetables to chop; linseed to boil; hay to fetch and nets to fill.

Micky whistled as he worked. This wasn't work; it was pure, undiluted pleasure. Whenever he needed a rest, he broke off and went outside to watch Mahruss. The stallion ran, the wind in his mane, full of pent-up energy. His hide gleamed with health.

Djeroua was being fed more often than the other two; her rations were quite different. So, Micky discovered later, was her nature. Where Trunca made him think about her by pulling his hair, Djeroua bent her head against him, and very gently, rubbed her muzzle against his cheek. Then, as he stroked her, rubbing her behind the ears, she took his hand in her mouth, nibbled softly, her eyes watching him all the time.

Raoul, as he brought the mare in for her mid-morning feed, looked about him approvingly. Micky had worked hard, and the stable was as well cleaned as if he had done it himself. He nodded approvingly.

The wall above Djeroua's stall held a picture of a different mare, almost as lovely. Beneath it, in Raoul's own language, was another piece of writing, beautifully lettered, and bordered with tiny, galloping foals.

'What does it say?' Micky asked.

'It is another saying of Mahommed, that "the Arabian horse is a creature without equal. He flies without

31

wings and he conquers without swords." There are so many stories of horses in my country. A man will teach his mare a secret word, so that when he races her, she will run faster than the wind and outrun every other mare. They are more precious than fine gems; more rewarding than any other creature. If we were in my own land, when the foal is born, he would be fed on the milk of my finest camel, so that when he grew up he would be stronger than any other foal.'

'You'd have problems getting camel's milk here,' Micky said, laughing.

He turned and looked at the Old Man. Grey clouds hid his head. The sky was yellow and angry at the edge of the cloud.

'There's going to be snow. Have we enough food if we get snowed in?'

'Food in plenty,' Raoul said. There was food for the horses in the shed behind the stables, hay in the barn. In the house he had two big deep-freezers as there was never time to shop, and he did not like cooking. He could not buy the food of his own country so had had to learn to live with the food in this new land of his. He longed at times for a different diet: for the sweet-meats his servants had cooked so well, for the syrupy coffee he loved; but a man in a strange land has little choice.

Micky went indoors to find out what he could cook, and took over all the catering. He cooked well, and enjoyed using foods that he had never had the money to buy. There was always something interesting if he burrowed deep. Raoul shopped extravagantly, used to the best of everything.

Snow came that night, but did not lie. By morning, there was only a faint memory on trees and hedges, and the grass was green again.

By the end of the week the pattern was set for the days to come; Micky spent the evenings clearing out the rubble from the cottage, eager to have a place of his own. He did not know what Raoul was doing.

Raoul was always busy: there were records to keep and orders for feed to make out; bills to pay, and it was time to think about furnishing the rest of the house and making a home. He had only furnished four rooms; his bedroom, the study, the kitchen and the little room that Micky used which he had hoped would have been his son's.

It was better to recognize the truth, and to learn to live with it. He could not bear the echoing rooms; it reminded him of a house that death had left deserted. Soon he would furnish his home. He would never go back now.

Micky could guard the horses while he drove to the big town to shop, instead of shopping by post: he would take his time. The boy would guard the horses with his life, of that Raoul was sure, and he would have Naseem to help him. The big dog followed either of them, unworried. He liked Micky who played with him, who hid things for the dog to find, and who was teaching him to hunt along a trail for hidden keys, or a handkerchief, or a piece of leather taken from the stables.

There were saddles and harnesses to clean; there was never time to be bored; in moments of leisure there was the stallion to watch, and endless hours to spend while Raoul trained the horse for dressage, sitting erect as if moulded into the animal, working on a passage, or beginning to train a piaffe in hand.

Micky had never seen advanced training. He longed to learn. He could ride as well as any jockey, and indeed had once wanted to be a jockey, but this was something else again. When Raoul lent him a book on dressage he pored over it endlessly, learning the terms, beginning to appreciate the delicate movements, the total control, the grace of the horse as he showed his paces, pride in every inch of his body.

Raoul would spend the whole of one session on a single movement, perfecting it, and Mahruss seemed to understand and do his best to please his master and match his enthusiasm.

It was an easy, pleasant way of life, although they were always very busy. Micky had never known such peace, or such pleasure; but it couldn't last. Nothing lasted, he had learned from experience far too young.

One night, when the moon was ringed with a strange halo, he looked up at it and shivered.

'Something is wrong?' Raoul asked, noticing the shiver, as he put the padlock on the mares' stable door.

'Ring around the moon. Me grandad said it meant bad luck,' Micky answered. 'Trouble ahead: maybe weather, maybe men.'

'I was always told it meant rain to come,' Raoul said. He looked up. The moon quivered through a halo-like haze of gold. He had never seen anything like it. He had seen other rings around the moon before, but not a ring like this.

Memories of his own people came back to Micky — omens and superstitions. He clutched the hare's foot in his pocket and stroked the stable door, touching wood for luck.

The wind whistled in the streets and another saying of his grandfather's came back to him.

'A windy night and a ringed moon, the witches ride, and the great hounds bay.'

Were there witches, he wondered, as he went indoors to prepare the meal. His grandfather had been sure of it and taken many precautions: a horseshoe of iron hung over the door; mountain-ash grew round the house; lucky charms and the crucifix that Micky's mother had given him long ago. The crucifix hung round Micky's neck now, under his shirt. He held it, asking protection, and then laughed at himself.

This was the nineteen-eighties; not the sixteen-eighties. The era of television, though that was never seen in this house. Raoul never had time to sit and watch, nor any desire to immerse himself in the strange stories of this country. The books on his shelves were all about horses; Micky had borrowed several, anxious

34

to learn all he could. One day he might have horses like these horses. One day he would ride a stallion like Mahruss.

Cooking supper, only half his thoughts on the meal, he drifted into a dream.

He was a king among men and he rode a stallion beyond price; a wonderful animal that put even Mahruss to shame. He rode him to perfection in front of a huge audience, an audience that gasped as he performed. Passage and piaffe; courbette and ballotade, his horse flying from the ground, every muscle tightened to perfect the movements. Voices roared applause.

Micky came back to earth as Raoul walked in, sniffing, commenting that the food was burning. Micky's face burned, too, as he remembered his daydream.

'What were you thinking about?' Raoul asked, his face amused.

'Caprioles and ballotades in hand,' Micky said.

And Raoul remembered how, as a boy, he had watched the Lippizaners train and he, too, had dreamed dreams.

CHAPTER FOUR

ANGHARAD, walking in the lanes, often watched Raoul training his stallion. He nodded to her, but never spoke, although she smiled. She did not want to intrude. Raoul shopped sometimes in the village shop, asking for all he needed, but he said very little. A quiet man, a reserved man, harming no one. The villagers admired his horses, but were a little afraid of him. He was a stranger and, coming from a world that none of them could imagine, was very different.

The farmers approved of the way he kept his horses. They admired them as the mares were led for exercise, or Raoul rode the stallion in the lanes. Nothing bothered Mahruss. He watched the traffic pass without flinching; he never shied, as other horses shied, at leaves blowing in the wind, or a weasel running across the road. His manners were impeccable.

Angharad loved the horse as she loved all animals. He came to her when he was alone in the field and dipped his muzzle into her hand. He liked the smell of her — a clean smell, of flower perfumes, that always clung about her. (Emily had told her mother once that Angharad smelled like a summer day.)

'When will the story of the horses start?' the children asked her.

'It has started. It is building. Everything takes time,' Angharad said. 'Time to grow, as you need time to grow. You are small now; one day you will be grown up, too; but it takes time. You can't hurry anything; time to walk the cattle home for milking; time for the dogs to herd the sheep on the hills; time for the mares to grow their foals and for the foals to be born.'

'Will there be foals?' the children asked.

'One foal, soon. Another foal near the end of the year,' Angharad said. 'You'll see. They will be very beautiful foals. They take longer than a human baby to grow inside their mothers. Everything needs time.'

The children had to be patient. They watched the mares and looked each day to see if the foals had come, but there was no sign of any foal.

Angharad listened to the wind on the slopes and watched the weather. One of the farmers in the valley referred to her as a weather-witch, and she laughed at him.

'Weather-wise,' she said. 'A witch would use the weather to do harm. I only tell you when to take the sheep in from the hills; when to move the cattle from the slopes; when the river will surge and foam down the village street. The Old Man is our only threat; we have no witches here. We don't need them, with him to hurl danger at us.'

'Do we need danger?' the children asked.

'Those who never know sorrow, can never value joy,' Angharad said. 'Those who are never cold will never crave for warmth; those who are never ill will never appreciate health. Those who never know danger will never know the peace that comes when danger has been banished. Seamen know it; the storms that threaten their ships and toss them on the waves die away, and there comes a balmy day of soft winds and warmth from the sun, and a still sea on which they can rest. Or they sail to harbour and come ashore, away from the winds and the storms, into the quiet of home, where children play, and fires warm the rooms, and there is good food and good company.'

The children, who had known no danger in their lives, listened to her wide-eyed. Sometimes she sang to them and told them of great cities where so many people walked that no one even knew the name of the man or woman next door; where there were so many children in the huge schools that no teacher could ever know all of them.

They were glad, then, of the village school where Dafydd Owen knew all of them by name, and knew their fathers and their mothers by name, too, and sent a tiny gift for a newborn brother or sister. His wife came to see the baby and brought one of the fragile lacy jackets that she loved to crochet. She made jackets for a store in London; they were very expensive to buy, but here they were given and treasured, and always worn when the baby was christened.

Bronwen Owen often sat with Angharad, sharing her fire's warmth, while they talked of the children and how they grew, and of the new babies born in the village. They talked of Cafell, walking the hills endlessly, and of the climber who had died on Nameless, his dog beside him. The dog would not leave the dead man's side and had to be dragged away. Cafell had howled on the wind all night. It was a wild night. The bereaved dog had howled, too.

They spoke of the man who had come to live on the hill and of his wonderful horses.

They spoke of the gipsy boy; Angharad took Bronwen with her when she went to renew the flowers on the Gipsy's grave.

'The boy came from nowhere,' she said. 'Did you see him come to the village?'

Bronwen smiled. Angharad loved mysteries; she loved the old stories; she loved all of them, and had a powerful imagination.

She saw the ring around the moon that Micky had seen, as she went out to call the cats in before going to bed. Both slept on her bed, Topsy curled into the small of her back, Polly nestling behind her knees. When she turned over in her sleep the cats moved too, keeping always to the warmth of their favourite places.

It was a wicked moon — a moon that promised danger.

High on the slopes of the Old Man Cafell was howling on the wind; the wind was whipping the snow; more snow would fall in the night. Not enough to threaten them; not enough to endanger them; not enough to account for the warning in the moon.

The moon vanished behind clouds so dense that the night was blackened at once, and the rain began.

The cats raced for the door, and Angharad closed it as they came in, and listened to the wild, wailing wind that whipped across the sky. She listened to the drumming of rain on the slate roof, to the beat of rain against her door, to the incessant wind that raced around the houses.

'Cafell is noisy tonight,' she said to the cats.

Uneasiness persisted. The rain would wash away the snow; but there would be danger from the rain: rain swelling the falls; rain swelling the brooks; rain flooding the fields; rain turning the little river, that in summer was so gentle, into a roaring flood that threw boulders on to the banks, that boiled and surged and thrust its way out of its bed, that cut new courses, that killed cattle and drowned sheep.

It could flood in a moment; it could sweep through the village street and soak the houses in mud; it could sweep people off their feet.

It had done so, years before. Would it do so tonight?

The rain lulled and the wind died, in a long, last whimper.

For all that there was more rain to come; perhaps more rain than the village had seen for years. She had seen a ring like that, long ago. She could not remember what it had foretold; there had been disaster. Not in their valley, but some miles away. Rain had fallen then, torrential rain.

She was growing old and her memory was betraying her. She needed to remember and perhaps she would avert disaster here. It would be here; she was sure of that. But not yet.

She dreamed often and her dreams told the future, though never clearly. She had to think, to work out what they meant. She had been dreaming of Cafell, yet he was not Cafell at all, but Naseem, the big German Shepherd that belonged to the stranger: and she had dreamed again and again of the gipsy boy even before he came to the village, which was why she made sure that the flowers on the Gipsy's grave were always fresh. She had dreamed of the horses.

She dreamed more as she grew older. She dreamed sometimes of swimming in the lake; of diving deep into the lake, and coming to a king's palace, more beautiful than any place she had ever seen.

There were green fields under the lake, and beautiful cattle. Blonde, blue-eyed girls with long hair met her and took her to their queen and garlanded her. Cafell sat waiting for her, and came to lick her hand. He was black, and more beautiful than any dog she had ever known.

It was warm there, under the lake and she felt as if she were going home. When she woke, though, she sometimes forgot the dream, the memory teased her, so that she was lonely, as if among strangers. Yet how could she be, for she had lived in the village all her life?

She could not remember her childhood clearly. It was too long ago. Yet she remembered her mother laughing at her, eyes blue, her hair long and shining. She remembered her father, a silent man who spoke little — small, dark, bearded — telling her the stories of the lake. Her mother had died when she was small.

The rain eased. The sky had cleared, but there was still a ring around the moon. A full moon; a hunter's moon; a moon that maddened the cats and dogs in the village. She could hear them baying now; one faraway voice sounded alone as if Cafell were calling his friends to him and the village dogs were answering. She knew all their voices.

Ben, the collie on the farm; Jamie, the collie/Alsatian cross that lived on the far side of the hills; Heidi, the little fawn bitch that owed her odd shape to a basset-hound mother and a labrador father, wriggling in affection, her sleek coat gleaming. Up on the hill Naseem joined in, his voice deep, sounding clearly through the night, and the stallion whinnied so that another another dog barked, and then the village was alive with barking dogs and men's voices shouting to them to be quiet.

The moon was gone, hidden behind the Old Man. The dogs were quiet. The only sound was that of one hound baying mournfully, a warning note in his voice; a soft call on the air as if the wind stirred round the houses. On the upper slopes of the Old Man the snow fell again, masking the rocks.

The rain began at dawn. The weather had changed during the night, and the village streets were sodden with slush when Angharad woke, very early, and fed her cats. She opened the door, but neither Polly nor Topsy would go outside. They leaned against her ankles and cried.

She looked up at the Old Man.

Snow covered the lower slopes, but the peak was hidden in massed cloud, cloud so dense that it darkened the sky and hid the rising sun. Lightning flashed, a jagged zip that arched towards the village. A moment later the thunder clap sent both cats scurrying under Angharad's bed. All she could see of them was two pairs of terrified eyes, glowering in the darkness. She closed the door.

The wind whistled outside. It was rising rapidly, rising to gale force, to hurricane force, bringing the rain with it. The sky was darker than night.

The rain began.

It lashed viciously out of the sky, drumming on the pavement, dancing in the gutters, falling against the windows in a continuous stream.

41

Up on the hill, the horses cried restively as lightning flashed again and again, and thunder rolled, echoing from the mountain peaks.

Naseem was restless, walking uneasily around the rooms, pushing against his master, asking for affection. Micky went to the horses, and was soaked as he raced across the yard.

Mahruss whinnied every time lightning flooded the sky, although the stable door was shut, and only the window let in the light. Micky masked the window with a sack, but lightning flashed under the door; lightning flashed at the edges of the sack and the thunder rumbled relentlessly.

The children could not reach the school. They would be soaked within seconds of opening the front doors. Babies cried and mothers hushed them, frightened, too. There had never been a storm like this in anyone's memory; not even Angharad's.

Rain continued all day; rain continued all night. By morning the first trickle of water was creeping up the village street. Gareth the Police went round the houses knocking on doors, warning people the time had come to find shelter. The church was on high ground but would not hold them all.

Angharad looked at the policeman, her face worried. 'We must ask all those with large houses on the hills to shelter us,' she said.

Gareth drove to all the big houses and made preparations for the people to take shelter, to bring their bedding and their food, their dogs and their cats. The cattle were walked to the high slopes; the sheep brought to the uplands. And everyone watched the river, for when it rained very hard, there was danger from the flood tide as well as from rivers springing from the faults of the Old Man, whose roaring could be heard above the sound of the falls.

Gareth came last to Raoul's house. Raoul met him, his face anxious.

'There is danger from flooding?' he asked.

42

Gareth nodded, not liking to ask a stranger among them to take in the people who would have to leave their homes; who would return to find the Old Man had ruined their possessions.

'Bring all those here who can come,' Raoul said. He led the way indoors. Gareth followed him, grateful.

'Most of the rooms are empty; they will need chairs and bedding, and something to lie on. Is there time?'

'Some time,' Gareth answered. 'Not much.'

He drove down the hill. The men loaded cars and lorries and vans, and even tractor trailers, taking everything they could from downstairs rooms. There were six families who would have to go to the house on the hill. They drove up, quiet, the children awed and frightened; the water was already creeping up the street. When the tide came to the full it would flood deep. There were marks high on the houses from floods long ago.

Micky came indoors. Angharad was one of the refugees. Raoul, who had himself left his own home, never to return, knew how they felt. He showed each family to an empty room. The house was huge by village standards, the rooms spacious.

Thomas Edwards, with his wife and six children, and the two cats and the budgerigar, was given the ballroom; the children had never seen so big a room in an ordinary house. They ran to the windows and looked out, down the valley to the village street, where the water now was over a foot deep.

Angharad was given a little room at the top of the house that had once been a dressing-room. There she put her mattress and a sleeping bag that Gareth had lent her. The two cats settled at once on the bag, warm, comfortable and unconcerned. Angharad had given them food as soon as they arrived.

She went downstairs to help with the children; to help Micky in the kitchen, to make plans for meals; to sort out the food that they had.

Everyone had brought food. Thomas Edwards' wife had been baking and had brought all she had made;

43

scones and Bara Brith and new brown loaves, fresh from the oven; two big cakes that were to have lasted the children for two weeks; and a huge pot of soup that was ready to cook and would serve many of them.

'If we add vegetables and dumplings and herbs . . .' Angharad said, and she and Micky chopped and diced carrots and turnips and potatoes that John Griffiths, from the farm higher on the hill, had sent down on his tractor, knowing they would need food. He had four families staying with him, and the lads had decided to camp in the barns. So long as no one had matches, John Griffiths agreed. Make the best of a bad job and let the lads have fun, was his thought to help counteract the misery.

The women were saddest; they thought of the cleaning that would be necessary when they went back; of the mud and the rocks that the Old Man would send to them; of the mess the water would bring to their houses; of ruined floors and ruined carpets and ruined decorations; of endless work in the weeks to come; and of all there was to do now.

Angharad did not give them time to think. She set them to work to make the rooms as comfortable as possible. From the hotel, which was soon to be unreachable except by water, Gwyn Owen arrived with his estate car piled high with bedding, and with the more precious ornaments from his wife's sitting room. Ten chickens were in the back of his wife's small car. Sian Owen laughed as she unloaded them into one of Raoul's stables.

'They will lay anywhere,' she said, bringing a huge basket of eggs with her as she came into the kitchen. She was a brisk, small woman, her usually neatly-waved hair now wet with rain, her eyes bright as she looked around her. She was used to cooking for climbers who stayed with her every year. Angharad at once yielded the catering to her, and left Sian with Micky, making lists of all the food they had.

'Never rains but it pours,' she said, and laughed as she set to slicing bread and buttering it.

44

Raoul, standing in his study with Naseem beside him, watching the rain falling again, saw how the rivers on the Old Man were racing fast down the slopes; racing towards the village, racing to consume the houses, racing to drown everything in their track. Sheep would die and cattle would die.

He was glad that he lived on a hill. The village was fully seventy feet below him and there were two farms above him. Their chimneys showed among the trees that protected them from the wind.

The wind was blowing strongly, keening around the house. One of the younger children cried.

'It is only Cafell,' Angharad said. 'He is protecting us. Aren't we lucky to be here? Warm and dry and with a big fire blazing . . . food to eat and a bed to sleep in and friends with us.'

Raoul had come into the room; he looked at Angharad, and she knew that he had no friends — a lonely man in an alien land.

'We are grateful,' she said.

'Don't be. It's the least I can do,' Raoul said. 'They are the sufferers.'

'We can repair the damage; and we will return to our own homes,' Angharad said. 'Yours is far away.'

Raoul led her to his study.

The fire blazed in the hearth and the big German Shepherd lifted his head; he growled at most people when first they came into the room, but he stood up and greeted Angharad, thrusting his nose into her hand.

'He favours you,' Raoul said.

Angharad looked about her. The shelves were lined with books; books on horses, horses from all over the world. There was one picture in the room: a picture of an Arabian stallion, not so beautiful as Mahruss.

The empty shelves at the far end of the room held tiny models of horses, each in perfect detail.

'Did you make those?' Angharad asked.

45

'I found some in a sale room,' Raoul said. 'Micky copied them and then began to make his own, using my horses as his models; he is very good.'

The tiny mare was only eight inches high. She cantered, mane and tail streaming, vibrant with movement. A stallion reared against the wall behind her, taller, magnificent, his body proud.

'You brought nothing from your own home?' she asked.

'I brought two horses, myself, and a few of my father's jewels to sell to give me money,' Raoul said. Memory was bitter. He did not want to remember. Better to think of the future and forget the past. That was gone, washed away as the village landmarks would be washed away. Tomorrow, if the floods subsided, it would be a different world for everyone.

It was strange to hear voices in this empty house that had been so quiet. Stranger, still, to hear children's voices. One of the younger women had once been a school teacher, and she had started the children singing. The adults joined in. They were all in the huge, family dining room that had nothing in it but an armchair, a small table and a large rug.

Raoul moved to the study window and pulled aside the curtain. Angharad had left him; Naseem was asleep, dreaming — perhaps of rabbits — his hind legs twitching and his tail beating as if he were eager to run. Raoul had never seen such rain in this country: rain that fell in cataracts from the sky; thunder that crashed with the noise of a thousand angry demons; lightning that flashed, danced and killed.

His fields looked unfamiliar, filled with sheep. Twenty heifers stood forlornly in the rain in the mares' pastures. Mahruss called to Raoul above the storm and he went out to the stable. The stallion was delighted to see his master; he hated this weather; he hated the wind and deafening thunder crash.

Raoul talked to him softly, stroking the stallion's neck. He filled the haynet, hoping the horse would eat and distract himself from the din. There was little he could do.

Padlocking the door again he walked across the yard; in moments his clothes were drenched; rain beat on the roof of the mares' stable. Djeroua was in the foaling box, so she could get used to it before the foal was born. He looked at Trunca first. She was wild-eyed and panting, but quietened when he touched her. Micky raced through the hail that now thudded down.

Lightning streamed across the sky, flashing again and again, sheets of brilliant, dazzling colour that blinded the eyes. Raoul pulled the door shut and stood soothing the mare as thunder echoed and rolled, and rolled again and again.

'I've never known anything like this,' Micky said.

'It will go,' Raoul said.

The echoes died, and he went outside and opened the door that led to the foaling box. Djeroua stood there, her flanks heaving, her hide wet with sweat.

She pawed the straw and Micky ran to her.

'She's starting to foal; it's early,' he said.

'Small wonder,' Raoul said. He walked over to the mare and felt along her side. 'It's lively enough.'

He moved fast as the lightning flashed again and the mare attempted to rear. He caught at her mane just as the lights went out.

'Power gone,' Micky said. 'I'll start the generator; but I'll bring you a lamp first. Better not leave her.'

'We dare not leave her,' Raoul said. His role would now be here in the stable, watching over the mare.

'Suppose we need the vet?'

It was a thought Raoul had not allowed to enter his head because he was pretty sure that something was amiss. He didn't know exactly what, but he had brought enough foals into the world to know that something was unusual. Maybe the foal lay wrong; maybe there were twins; maybe the mare was unwell. There was worry in her eyes, and the droop of her head bothered him.

Micky brought in a handlamp and vanished again to fight the big engine that ran the generator. One of the farmers came to help him. Soon lights came on again in the house, and dimly in the stable, but not sufficient light.

They needed light.

If only the rain would ease, but now it was drumming even harder on the stable roof. The thunder seemed to be closer, seemed to be all around them, as if the Old Man roared with anger at them; as if he hated all of them and would destroy them if he could.

It was worse than a desert storm when the sand was whipped into tormenting devils that stung and covered and choked those caught in them.

Micky came back, his clothes clinging to him, his wet hair flattened on his head. Rain ran down his chin.

He handed Raoul a thermos flask filled with soup, and a large biscuit tin in which were sandwiches, cakes and fruit. There were also two plastic mugs.

'Someone's been busy,' Raoul said, marvelling that anyone could produce such things so quickly.

'One of the children was going to have a birthday party tomorrow; his mother put in the picnic things she had bought knowing they would be useful. The village has had floods before; people take precautions.'

They felt marooned in the stable. Raoul ate absent-mindedly, his hands quick to reach out to the mare. She tossed her head, eyes wild, and stamped in the straw.

Raoul had never had a problem with a foal before. There was a bad problem this time. Micky watched the mare anxiously. Suppose she died, or the foal died?

Thunder crashed. There was a sudden tremendous crack, a gun roar.

'Tree hit somewhere near,' Micky said. It was no use looking out. There were no trees near the house. An animal might be harmed. The heifers were lowing and the sheep bleating. Above the storm noise and the howl of a dog sounded another noise. Micky suddenly realized it came from the heronry at the edge of the mares' field; herons screamed in fear, and then the twitter and alarm calls of other birds echoed through the storm.

The wind tormented the trees so that they, too, cried as though they were being tortured.

Children were crying in the house. There were women enough to quieten them. Voices rang out in song, blending with the wind and the rain and the thunder rumble that was dying away.

Mahruss whinnied, loud and long; Trunca echoed him. Naseem raced through the storm. He had been pawing at the back door, desperate to reach his master, and Rhian Edwards, who was fifteen, had let him out. He was soaked, but he was safe. He settled in the straw, watching the mare as if he understood her agony.

Gareth the Police put his head round the door.

'Trouble?' he asked. There wasn't a man in the village who didn't know about animals; most of them kept a few cattle, some only to rear for beef; some for milk and butter, to help with the family budget. Each cottage had its own little garden and some had paddocks where cattle could feed.

'Trouble,' Raoul said.

'We can never get the vet. We're cut off by water; it's all around us now. And the Old Man has dropped a few tons of rock at the far end of the village street; luckily it hasn't harmed the houses. It will have to be shifted before anything can get through to us, though.'

Raoul looked at his mare. She was to found his fortune in this new land; her foal was to bring him a new way of life — a new occupation. Her foal was to be sold and make his mother famous. Raoul would only keep the foal if it were a filly foal; he would sell a stallion.

But he did not care what the foal might be at the moment. Djeroua meant more to him than wealth. He stroked her soft neck, but she had no eyes for him.

49

She was immersed in her own pain; and he had no way of relieving it.

Micky offered her water, but she would not drink.

The door opened. Angharad came in. Gareth had gone to tell her of the mare's distress.

'I have helped with babies and with lambs and with calves,' she said. 'Can I help now? It might be her only chance.'

'She is already in milk,' Raoul said.

Djeroua ignored them all. She was covered in sweat, and had dropped to the ground, where she rolled, and then stood again. Micky went to her head, and took her halter. He led her gently round the box, talking to her, whispering to her, whistling softly, while Raoul and Angharad watched closely.

The dim light was a nuisance but there was nothing they could do about it. The generator thudded in the background, adding its noise to the storm. So long as it kept going and there was enough fuel . . .

'I've brought you fuel for the generator,' a voice said softly from the doorway. It was Huw Owen, the farmer from the highest farm on the hill. 'I've extra lights. Gareth said you were in trouble.'

Raoul took the lights. The voice had been soft so as not to alarm the mare further. There were four powerful handlamps, and they flooded the room with welcome brightness. Angharad was washing her hands at the basin. The mare was down again, but there was no sign of the foal.

Thunder rumbled in the distance. The children's voices sounded from the house singing 'All Through the Night', in Welsh. Raoul looked at his watch. It was just before midnight. No one could sleep tonight, except for the babies. Singing kept fear at bay.

It had been a long day and it was now obvious that it would be a still longer night.

Angharad knelt beside the mare, her voice soothing and soft. Her hands were gentle; her face absorbed, blue eyes intent. The mare's heavy breathing and the rustling straw were the only sounds in the stable, but outside, echoing, the thunder rolled again and the mare stood, and once more tried to rear.

'Acushla, baby,' Micky said.

'Softly, little girl,' said Raoul, in his own tongue. He was only half aware that he had slipped back to other days, to another time, when he had stood beside other mares, and outside the desert sand had been burnished by a glowing sun; or a brilliant moon had lighted the desert, and the stars above were brighter than any he saw here. The sand swept wide and clean in front of him, ridged and pocked by the whispering wind. The mare at his feet became all his other mares, and he was back in time waiting, with his wife, for news of the foal; and the boy, his eyes shining with excitement, was creeping out to stand beside his father.

'Will it be a colt or a filly?'

Micky's voice brought Raoul back to reality; back to the stable under the shadow of the Old Man, back to the flooded village street and the children singing in a language he could not understand at all, back to Angharad who was also talking in her own tongue to the mare, soothing her, gentling her, reassuring her.

It would have to happen tonight.

'Can we save the foal?' Raoul asked.

Angharad looked up at him.

'I am not even sure that we can save the mare,' she said. 'The foal has twisted inside her. We should have a vet, but no vet can reach us tonight; it is up to us. Have you ever brought a foal that was laid wrongly?'

Raoul shook his head. He had been lucky, all those years; only once had there been trouble and then he had had a stable groom who was a genius with horses — far cleverer than any vet that Raoul had ever met.

'I will try,' Angharad said. 'I will need help; but I can promise nothing.'

Outside, in the dark, the wind howled, thunder roared, and water gushed from the Old Man's slopes. The flood in the village street grew deeper.

Rocks slipped from their places; and high on the hill, beyond the sound of the thunder, was a crying and a calling.

'Cafell is watching,' Angharad said, and bent her head to the mare.

CHAPTER FIVE

RAOUL, holding the mare's head, was once more back in another world. He had stood like this so often in his own land, beside so many mares. Nothing had changed. The smell of horses; the feel of the straw under his feet; the movements of the mare as she tried to give birth. The intent head of the woman working on her was the only difference. Women did not work with horses in his own land, though his wife had always come to see the new foals and brought the boy with her.

The loneliness that he carried inside him, always, was appeased. This was the same everywhere in the world, wherever horses were bred. The mating, the training, the feeding, and the foaling; the baby that staggered on wobbly legs, looking up trustingly at the people around him, at his mother, at this new world. A world of white-washed walls, and straw beneath his hooves, and gentle voices.

Micky brought coffee and sandwiches for all of them, which had been made in the house.

Raoul came back to the present; to the knowledge that his home was now a refuge for strangers; that it housed very many, instead of just himself and Micky; the knowledge that his fields were full of unhappy beasts, trying to shelter from the rain and the driving wind.

The wind was moaning softly, sorrowfully.

'Cafell is noisy tonight,' Angharad said. Her eyes were on the mare as she drank her coffee.

'Cafell?' Micky said.

'Cafell was Arthur's hound, long ago,' Angharad said. 'He protected the king all his life; and he has protected our village ever since. Once this was known as Arthur's place; but the old name is forgotten. The great hound keeps climbers from danger, if they will only follow him; and his voice is heard on the wind, telling us he is guarding us and that all will be well.'

'I have heard of Cafell,' Micky said. 'I met an old man by the grave that is always covered in flowers, out beyond the village. The wind was making a terrific din; he said it was Cafell.'

'By the Gipsy's grave?' Angharad asked. She looked at Micky. 'Did you know it was called that?'

Micky shook his head.

'A boy came to this village, long ago,' Angharad said. 'He was cold and he was starving, and he had no friends. He was taken in by one of the farms, and tended the cattle. He was wonderful with animals, as all gipsies are. He said he had been sent to save the village from harm, but nothing ever happened in his lifetime. When he was dying, he told those around him to see that his grave stood alone, at the entrance to the village; that it was always tended and always remembered, and then, when the hour of need came, he would return and save the village. His time had come and gone; but in another time, still to come, he would be there.'

'Did he ever come back?' Micky asked.

Angharad turned away as she bent again to the mare.

'Not in the years that passed,' she said.

Micky looked out at the night; there were no stars; the rain was easing, but the wind still drove past the houses, keening softly like a whimpering pup, and then suddenly strong again, baying at the night, howling through the trees, as if indeed it were a living thing.

'If I had a dog I would like to name it Cafell,' Micky said. 'It's a good name.'

Naseem was standing at the doorway, his ears pricked, growling deep in his throat.

There were footsteps in the yard.

Gareth the Police stood in the doorway, and Raoul quieted the dog.

'I must go now,' Gareth said. 'Everyone is well and Sian has fed them all. Some of the women are baking; they will replace your food when the danger is over and we are back to normal again. My wife is with John Griffiths up the hill.'

'Take care,' Angharad said.

'Cafell will guard me.' He smiled at her, and was gone, his footsteps dying away in the darkness. Naseem returned to Raoul's side and dropped into the straw.

'Will it be long?' Micky asked, watching the mare, wishing with all his heart that he could help her and bring the foal quickly. She had gone away from them into her own world and was aware of nothing but her pain.

'The foal has one leg curled beneath him; that is why he won't come,' Angharad said. 'I will have to work to straighten it; please God I can.'

Raoul knew that if she couldn't both mare and foal would die.

He would lose the mare that he loved more than his life; his link with the past, his hope for the future. He stood beside her, caressing her head, but she was unaware of him.

Naseem butted his master's leg jealously.

'I have not forgotten you,' Raoul said, in his own tongue. It fitted the time and the night and the stable. The wind outside was the desert wind; the yard outside had gone and beyond were the desert sands and the high sky above him; his own men busy with their affairs, and his camel drivers attending to his camels. For the queen of the camels would provide milk to rear this foal.

When the foal was born he would write out a birth certificate in the old way. He had a parchment that he had found in an antique shop, the paper yellowed, the words almost unreadable; he would copy that. This foal would be treated as a king in his own right from birth.

In his own land the sheikhs always took the foal and worked on it; to give it life and strength and to teach it to love man.

Angharad was hissing softly under her breath, her hands busy. She, too, spoke in her own tongue. Raoul could understand English but he could not understand Welsh.

Micky was whispering under his breath, a prayer that went on endlessly to the God he had been taught about when he went to school — a child's prayer, repeated like a talisman — 'Please God, don't let her die' — over and over, the words giving him some comfort.

Raoul settled in the straw, holding the mare's head against him. She was lying now, resting, but her wild eyes and sweat-drenched coat told their own story.

He dared not think about her. He whispered to her softly and tried to fill his mind with other thoughts. Then, unbidden, came the memory of a day long ago when he had been younger than Micky and had been taken with the camel train on a desert journey. He could not remember where, or why.

The wind howled round the stable and whipped the straw, but Raoul was on the back of a magnificent cream camel, caparisoned in silver, blue and gold. The camel train stretched behind him and in front of him, and the sun beat down on them, casting odd shadows that dipped and swayed as the camels walked.

A turbaned man in long robes led his camel. His father rode behind, a fierce old man with fierce dark eyes, grey hair and a grey beard, and a great gentleness towards his son and towards his horses.

The sand was rippled and pockmarked by the wind; a little wind that stroked his face, but that yesterday had screamed along the ground, sending up spirals of dust high into the air, changing the shape of everything around them. They had been forced to shelter for a long time.

The sand was blown into buttresses; little cliffs rose around them as they journeyed on; strangely shaped peaks mocked them, and they changed their path.

And then Raoul remembered why they had made the journey.

They had come by night into a city of tents, where they were met by an old man, so old that even his father looked young beside him. He led them to another tent where a mare stood with her new foal.

He had never seen such a mare. He had never seen such a foal. Not even among his father's horses; and his father was famous for the horses he bred.

He had gasped, and the old man had looked at him through eyes that seemed to bore into his soul.

'Your son recognizes worth,' the old man said. 'You taught him well, my friend. The mare is for him?'

How could he have forgotten? The mare had been his birthday gift from his father; and the foal came, too. The foundation of his own breeding stock, bringing new blood into the horses. She had been Djeroua's great-grandmother.

That night they had feasted; and he slept in a strange tent and listened to the sounds of men singing late into the night as the camel men feasted, too.

In the morning, mare and foal had joined their cavalcade.

'Remember,' the old man said, 'her mother drank of the desert wind. Her sire outstripped the gazelle. Treasure her and guard her well; she is dearer to me than life; yet I let her go, as I am an old man now and I have no son to take my horses and treasure them as I do. You are a fortunate man,' he had said to Raoul's father.

Raoul had prized her, but not so much as he prized her great-grand-daughter.

In those far away days the world had seemed safe and secure; he imagined he would go on as his father had gone on, and reign in their little country and rule well; he would marry and have a son, and his son would reign after him and their horses would be famous throughout the world. But his world had ended on a bright morning when his cousin fired a gun.

Raoul opened his eyes as Micky shook his arm urgently.

'Are you all right? You shouted . . .'

'I was dreaming,' Raoul said.

Angharad turned her head and looked at him, and he wondered if those vivid eyes could read his mind.

'Birth and death are the same the world over,' she said.

Far away the thunder rumbled and above it came another sound — a terrifying roar, louder than anything they had heard, louder than the thunder and louder than the wind.

'The Old Man is throwing rocks again,' Angharad said. 'Please God that nobody is in the way.'

'A landslide?' Micky asked, listening to the awful sounds from outside.

'We are safe here; others may not be.'

Angharad had her mind on the mare. Raoul stood beside her. He gave a soft, pleased sigh.

A moment later the mare heaved her sides and the foal came free.

'I'll see to the mare. You look after the foal,' Angharad said. It was hard to make herself heard above the tremendous roar outside.

Micky was already moving the mare to the next stall where clean straw awaited her.

Raoul took the foal.

This he had done before so often in his own country. The feeling of familiarity reassured him more than anything else had done in the past months. He had a home again; and this was part of his home.

This was so familiar. Cleaning the foal, cleaning away the membrane; holding the small head, and watching the first breath; the first twitch of the ears; the widening of small nostrils; the first sneeze; the first tiny whicker that brought the mare to her feet, her eyes looking around for it, knowing the sound although she had never heard it in her life, this being her first foal. She was looking for it, so intently, that Raoul brought the foal to her, and held it against her.

She bent her head and sniffed it, smelling from tail to head and back again. Her tongue came out and she began to lick it clean. Raoul stroked her neck and she turned to look at him and nudge him, moving towards her foal.

'She knows she's clever,' Micky said.

He, too, had slipped back in time, to his grandfather's stables. One night a bought-in mare had foaled; but not such a foal as this.

It was exquisite, a tiny replica of its mother, a filly foal.

She tried to stand on legs that refused to hold her, and slipped back into the straw. Djeroua nudged her, and Raoul helped the baby to stand and guided her head to the first milk, the milk that was needed to bring strength and give her immunity against the many diseases that threaten young lives.

Angharad cleaned the mare, and Micky brought water and bran mash.

They had forgotten the wildness of the night, but now, as the mountains rumbled again and the thunder of falling rocks echoed through the valley, the generator coughed and died once more, and they were left with only the light of the handlamps.

'Will you give her an Arab name?' Angharad asked.

'This is my home now,' Raoul said. 'I will give her a name that suits her country.'

'Then name her Rhiannon, for Rhiannon is the goddess of horses,' Angharad said. 'It will be lucky for her.'

Micky had gone to look at the generator.

The mare whinnied and the baby answered, and from the next stable came the voice of Mahruss answering, as if he knew that this foal was his, too.

Raoul, kneeling by the foal, looked at her carefully. The hair grew oddly on either side of her neck. 'She has both Mohammed's thumb marks,' he said. 'She will be very beautiful — and very lucky.'

Angharad looked at the marks, which were tiny whorls in the hair.

'We will need luck,' she said, listening to the wildness outside.

'I wish I could tell my bees,' Angharad said, and thought of the hives, there in the flooded garden, perhaps buried under part of the mountain.

Outside the stable, lightning flashed again.

The mare ignored everything but the foal.

'She will do now,' Angharad said. 'We will look at her again in an hour. Let her get to know her foal.'

They took a handlamp each and walked towards the house, and as they crossed the yard the generator started up again and lights came on. The roar from the hills was greater; there was a sound of tumbling rock and the terrifying sound of moving water; more water than any of the villagers had ever seen before.

Raoul went to look at the stallion and to quieten Trunca; Micky put them together in one stable, in adjacent stalls; they could comfort one another. He went to the house, where most of the refugees now slept. Sian sat in the kitchen, and poured coffee for them, cut bread, and heated soup.

It was very early in the morning when Raoul went to his room and stretched out on the bed. Micky would keep watch, and could sleep later on.

Inside the stable the mare lay with the foal tucked against her and slept, too, but woke when the baby moved, and looked at it as if unable to believe that this was hers.

The foal had come into a world that had changed overnight; but nobody knew that till morning came and the sun rose, dim, over a village that had vanished under rock — so much rock that no one would ever see their homes again.

CHAPTER SIX

RAOUL was up at first light to look at the foal. The world was still dark. The rain had eased, but there was an unfamiliar background sound that was different — the sound of rushing water. He had never heard that before.

The mare was on her feet, the baby feeding. Raoul watched them. Djeroua pushed her head against him telling him that nothing had changed between them. The foal looked up at him through wide, wondering eyes, but she was hungry; she had just learned to stand without falling and she was intent on drinking.

It was very quiet in the yard, except for the sound of roaring water. An owl flew by, his wings beating a slow rhythm. He was a familiar sight in the yard, flying every evening just before dusk from his nest in the old barn high up on the hill, at the farm above Raoul's home.

Angharad came into the stable, having paused in the doorway to watch the owl.

'They do well,' Raoul said.

Angharad stroked the mare's neck, and looked down at the foal. She was beautiful; tiny, elegant, perfect, a fairylike creature, suddenly huffing up at the man and the woman before returning to feed.

Someone inside the house was singing, a soft, lilting voice that was lifted happily.

'It is Sian getting the breakfast for us all,' Angharad said. 'She always sings as she works.'

'What is that noise?' Raoul asked. He was peering into the dark. Light was faint in the yard.

'I do not like to guess,' Angharad said. 'We will see, only too clearly, when it is lighter. There is nothing we can do now. Let us go and eat.'

Sian had made quantities of porridge. There was very little water, but there was plenty of milk. There were forty cows in the horse pasture; and nowhere to take the milk at all. Three of the men had been up early and there was milk in every bucket and milk in every jug; there was milk in two washing-up bowls, and milk outside in the horse trough — milk for everybody.

'We can cook in milk, and drink milk, and wash in milk if we must,' Sian said. 'We can live on milk for a long time if it's necessary.'

'If only it doesn't rain again,' Dick Morris said, coming into the room. He was an Englishman who had retired to Wales and kept the little shop in the village street. His grey hair stood straight on end, no matter how he brushed it. His wife cut it for him, and he often teased her about her lack of skill. Mary, his wife, followed him into the room.

'It's terrible,' she said. 'But maybe in a day or two we can go home.'

Raoul was gazing through the window. He looked down on more water than he had ever seen before, streaming down the mountain, streaming through what had once been the village street. There was no sign of houses. Here and there great boulders showed above the water.

Angharad joined him. All she could think of was her bees, drowned in their hives; her garden gone, as well as her herbs and flowers and roses.

Raoul did not know what to say. Their world had vanished as surely as had his own. He had his horses; some of these people had their cattle and their sheep; the rest had nothing. But at least they were all alive.

'Life is what matters,' he said suddenly and fiercely to Angharad.

She looked at him — a long, considering look.

'I know,' she said. She turned to those in the room. 'Come and look.'

They stared down at the water; no one could speak; no one had words for such a disaster. There were tears on Mary's cheeks, and Sian's face was white. Dick Morris put an arm round his wife's shoulders.

'At least the cat is alive,' he said, and Mary laughed, but it was not amused laughter.

'We must eat,' Raoul said, breaking into the noise sharply, and Sian turned to the table and began to spoon out the porridge onto plates. There were not enough plates for everyone to eat at once; they would have to eat in turn.

The old kitchen was big enough for everyone; soon it was filled with silent people; the children stood at the window, eating from mugs and cups, unable to believe their eyes.

'We can't go to school,' little Dai Evans said, watching the water. He wondered where his house was — there under all the rock. His new puppy was safe upstairs in the room where he and his parents had slept. His baby sister slept there too, tucked in blankets in an empty drawer from Raoul's chest.

Micky looked down from his bedroom window, and came — tousle-haired — into the kitchen, pulling a jersey over his head.

Sian spooned porridge into a small, milk saucepan and handed it to him.

He looked at it and grinned at her.

'Beggars can't be choosers,' he said, feeling a need to say something, to say anything, knowing how these people must feel. They would feel as he did when his grandfather died and he lost the horses; the only creatures he had ever truly needed. They would feel as Raoul did when he came to this country, from whatever foreign land had once been his. Like him, they had nothing, but they were in their own land — among their own friends.

Raoul was a foreigner in a strange land; and Micky himself was a gipsy, and hardly anyone sympathized with the gipsy people.

When breakfast was over, everyone drifted off to their rooms. Nobody knew what to do or what to say. Raoul went to feed the mare and Micky to clean out her stall.

'What are we going to do?' Micky asked.

'Hold a council of war when they have had time to recover a little from the shock,' Raoul said. 'There's room here for all those who are with us now. The men can get to work on the cottage; that will take one family. There are rooms above the stables where another family can live. There is plenty of room for Angharad in the house; she only needs two rooms; the Morrises, too, could manage with two big rooms; there are twenty rooms in that house, and I only use four of them. You can keep your little room for the time being. But we need to think about food for the next week or so. There is not enough fuel for the generator; and there isn't a road any more.'

'Helicopters,' Micky said, thrusting the pitchfork deep into the straw as if he were thrusting it into the Old Man who had ruined so many lives overnight. He pushed the barrow across to the midden and went to the wall of the first field and looked over.

Water thrust its way over the ground well below him, surging and racing, branches, and pieces of furniture, tossing on the brown foam. Beyond the path of the water that ran along what had once been the village street, the sides of the Old Man reared, gaunt and unfamiliar. All the loose soil and rock from the slopes had been washed away by the fury of last night's torrential storm, so that rock cliffs reared high above the street, sheer to the sky, a gaping wound that would never heal. There would never be trees on that rock face; not even the snow would lie.

Micky took the barrow and pushed it back to the stable.

The foal turned to him, butting him in the chest.

'You little monkey,' he said, and stroked her between the ears. She had already learned to love and trust people. One of the smaller boys stood in the doorway and Micky beckoned him in.

'Move slowly,' he said. 'Don't worry Djeroua. She might kick.'

'It's lovely,' the boy said. 'What's its name?'

'Rhiannon,' Angharad said, from the doorway. 'Micky, Raoul wants you; there's a meeting in his study. We have to decide what to do, and how to do today's work. Nobody can leave here yet. There is no road and nowhere to go.'

Micky went into the house.

The study seemed packed, mainly with men. The big wood stove had been lit, and the door stood open, revealing a comforting blaze. It was the only room that Raoul had troubled to furnish. Firelight danced on the books; danced on the pictures of horses and on the statues of horses on the shelves; reflected in the windows, that were still dark.

'We're going to get snow,' Dick Morris said. It was an added worry. They needed food; they needed clothes and bedding; there was not enough to live on — only for an emergency — and nobody had expected the emergency to be permanent.

'There is a home for everyone here,' Raoul said into the silence. Faces turned to look at him. 'It will take time to sort out what you all wish to do. Time to find new houses. Time to rebuild. And if the waters go down, would it be wise ever to build in the valley again? I started life again only a few months ago with nothing except my life and my horses. You have your lives and your families and your beasts safe with you.

'We need shelter; and we have shelter. We need food, and that can be arranged. We need to furnish the rooms, and when this weather eases, we can manage that, somehow. We can work here; and those who have jobs in the town can get there, when the weather

65

improves. Those who had work in the village will have to find other work. Until then let's start by dividing the house. A home can be made over the stables; the cottage behind the barn can be redecorated. The big barn would make an excellent home. You can pay me rent when your lives begin again. Meantime, we need the children to collect wood; there is plenty in the two coppices behind the barns; there is cleaning and cooking to be done to make us comfortable; and work on the buildings, and with the animals.'

'My black cow is in calf,' Huw Morgan said.

'Bring her into the end stall in the stable and keep her there.' Raoul had purpose again in life. He knew how it felt to lose everything and to despair. Now he could help these people; he had a place to offer them. He could offer them time — time to recover; time to rebuild; time to make new lives.

'Nothing will be the same again,' Dick Morris said. He thought of his little shop, buried under the water. It had been well-stocked; a place for people to come daily, to buy, to chat, or just to laugh in. He had been a great man for a joke, but he felt now as if every joke in his head had gone for ever.

'Work,' Raoul said, knowing work would help them to recover.

The children were given bags to fill with kindling. Dick Morris and Huw Morgan took the chain saw and went to cut down small trees and saw them into logs. Sian looked around the kitchen, and she and Angharad made a list of all the food they had. It would not last them long.

There was a rattle at the door, and Owen Pritchard, from the top farm on the hill, came into the kitchen, shaking rain from his cap.

'Aiee, it's a bad day for us all,' he said. He held out his hands to the Calor gas fire. 'It's wickedly cold; too cold for snow, which is one good thing.'

'That's true,' Angharad said. 'How many people have you up there, Owen?'

'Four families. Mair sent down food for you, knowing how it would be. We always stock up very well for winter. We can be cut off for weeks. If someone could get round the head of the water and find a place to telephone . . . All our lines are down. They'd send a helicopter with food for us. We could make a list of all we needed. There's two sacks of potatoes on my tractor. And there's eggs in plenty as I can't get mine to market; there's forty dozen I had packed and ready to go today; I've brought you twenty dozen. You've milk in plenty. Maybe you could spare us some? I've no cattle. Only sheep; too high for cows there on the hill. They never thrive in winter.'

'We can give you milk,' Sian said. 'We're bathing in it; more than we know what to do with.'

'Enough to spare for us, too? I've three families up there at Glanllyn,' Mark Hunter said, coming into the room. He bred horses on the other side of the hill. Nearly everyone had forgotten him. His Welsh ponies were famous in the local show, carrying off all the prizes.

Naseem came to him and sniffed his trousers, going over every inch.

'Smells my bitch,' Mark said. 'I've brought two churns from old Evan Williams. He's too rheumaticky to come down; he has two more families with him; Gareth was clever, getting everyone out like that. No lives lost at all.'

'Have you food?' Sian asked, assessing the eggs, the milk, and potatoes. They could eat baked custards till they looked like them; and she had found a store of apples that Micky had put away in the attic, wrapped in paper; enough for a few days, cooked, with custard. They could kill their own meat if they had to.

'I think we'd better empty all the freezers,' Raoul said. 'The generators can't keep everything going; if we divide up the meat and the food in there between us all and cook it, it will keep a day or two and by then surely they will find a way to drop us food.'

67

'My 'phone's dead; and we've no water or electricity,' Mark said.

'The well at my house is deep and we use it all the time,' Owen Pritchard said. 'I can bring water down on the tractor. I've spare tanks that we can lend you; I always said they would come in handy one fine day!'

Micky was looking out of the window, trying to work out if he could possibly get across the valley to the other side, and find a path to the next village where they might still be in touch with the world. The only radio that Raoul owned ran off the mains. The battery in Micky's transistor radio needed changing, and no one else had thought to bring such an item with them.

Raoul and Angharad made a list of all the people in the house. Then they went through the house. There were six families, two of them with young children.

'We can turn the ballroom into a room for everyone,' Raoul said. 'Make it a room to meet in, or to watch television; a room where families can sit and talk together. We can build a playroom for the children in the big barn; the rafters are sound and will take a swing for the little ones. There are two rooms together that would make a home for you — a large bedroom with a big dressing room beside it. Once, I think, the master of the house slept there. There is another smaller room with a room leading off it which would make a home for the Morrises. At least till they find somewhere to go,' he added. It did not do to make plans for other people.

'It sounds wonderful,' Angharad said. 'I would hate to leave the valley now; I was born here and I hope to die here. Perhaps I could plant a garden and keep bees when we are all settled; my bees died when the village was flooded.'

She minded losing the bees more than she minded losing her house and her furnishings. It would be easy to replace the bees, but they had been living creatures that she had cherished, feeding them in winter, taking

68

off the honey in summer; telling them of the joys and sorrows of the village. They had played a major part in her life.

'I think someone should try and get in touch with the village on the other side of the Old Man,' she said, pushing the thought of her loss out of her mind. Small, unbidden thoughts kept coming to her; the little table that had been her mother's, that she had polished lovingly every day; the Welsh crocheted patchwork bedspread that her grandmother had made which could never be replaced; the pretty china in her cupboard that she had had all her life, given her by a favourite great-aunt; her books, many of which were now out of print and could not be bought anywhere.

All of the refugees from the village had lost a lifetime of treasures. One small girl was crying bitterly for her new rag doll, dressed in ribbons and lace, beautifully made by her godmother specially for her birthday. Angharad would find ribbons and lace and make her another, when there was time; but it would never be the same.

Mary Morris paused, wiping away tears from her eyes.

'These old onions,' she said crossly.

She went on chopping, the sharp sound vicious on the board, as if she were chopping away anger at everything that had happened.

'It isn't the shop I mind,' she said, as Angharad joined her, and took up a knife to peel potatoes. 'It's the little things — the silly things. My grand-daughter painted me a picture; it was a terrible picture, but I loved it because she did it just for me. And the opal ring that Dick gave me for my birthday when I was sixteen, long before we married; only a cheap ring, but it was so pretty and when we were engaged I didn't want another ring; that was my engagement ring. Forty years. It's been a long time. So much has happened; and yet I can't believe it's so long. The years fly by and everyone else looks older, but you never feel older than yesterday.'

She laughed and took another vicious chop at an onion.

'How could you? The years creep on, minute by minute; and you work and plan and suddenly the children have gone and you are on your own again, looking forward to being together, to doing something you wanted to do all your life. A little shop in a little village, in the mountains, Dick used to say when we were young. It came true; for a little while. Now, it's all gone.'

She went out of the room, and Angharad took over the onions.

'Soup,' Sian said. 'We have carrots and turnips and potatoes; we have meat to put in it; we have flour for bread; and we will soon have water. We have all we need.' But her voice was desolate. She looked out of the window.

'So sudden,' she said angrily. 'Last week, we were all safe, all planning for the summer, talking about the seeds we wanted; making out lists of vegetables to grow in the garden; buying fertilizer, and putting it on the land; planning shows for the sheep, and shows for the goats; and an entry for our big, beautiful Jacob ram — mean old thing he is with his butting horns. Now, it all seems unimportant; nothing to plan for any more. It was more of a farm than a hotel.'

'Summer will still come,' Angharad said.

The children came in with bundles of wood; they were flushed with cold and damp with rain and their hands were dirty. Sian sat them down in a row on the floor and started to heat milk for cocoa. Raoul had a very well-stocked pantry and Micky loved cocoa. The shops were so far away that everyone shopped by the month. Sian thought of her own stores, carefully put away; the pounds of jam she had made in summer; the pickles and the chutney; the mint and cranberry jellies — all swept away in the torrent.

The children had grouped themselves by the big window. It was frightening, but it was exciting; they wondered where the school lay; where the shop was; nothing would be the same any more. The village street was one long gash of water, foaming and boiling.

'Will the water ever go?' little Annette asked, but no one could answer her. Sian was lost in her own thoughts; Angharad had gone to check the mare and foal, as Raoul was busy with the men. They were working on the cottage, planning to make it into a home for Annette's family. Micky had cleared everything out but the roof needed mending and every room had to be cleaned and decorated.

The road had gone, vanished, like the village, under water. The lane from Raoul's house led into twenty yards of tarmac that disappeared into the torrent. The lane wound round to the other farms on the hill and went nowhere. They were totally isolated.

'Where did Gareth go?' Micky asked at lunchtime.

The policeman had been busy helping everyone to move out of their homes; he had been to and fro several times, but nobody had seen him for more than twelve hours, and Dick Morris, when lunch was finished, decided to walk to the other farms, and on to Glanllyn, to ask if anyone knew what had happened to him.

He found Gareth's young wife at Glanllyn, with her cat and her budgerigar, and Jack Russell, Abbie. Megan's face was white with worry.

'He'll be safe,' Dick said, but wondered as he left. Gareth had not been to any of the other farms. Nobody had seen him. Perhaps he had gone for help across the hills.

Nothing could stop the children's excitement; everything was strange, but everything was interesting — from the new foal in the stable to the big, empty rooms in which they were now living. It was such an odd house, a huge house, built there on the hill long ago by a very rich merchant with a large family of daughters, and servants to run it. He had built stables and coach-houses, and cottages for his staff, as well as rooms over almost every barn and outhouse. As the

71

children explored, more and more was discovered. There was room for half the village here.

Raoul had never explored in such detail as the children. They were looking for treasure, but found nothing but cobwebs and owl droppings. The barn owl, indignant at their intrusion, terrified them by a sudden furious hiss and so they left him in peace.

They had been told not to go to the stables or disturb the mare, but they were allowed in the rooms above the stables. There were interesting old tools in the big barn. Dafydd Owen found an ancient mangle with huge rollers and a handle that none of them could turn.

Micky, coming into the barn to look for his hay rake, sent them out again in case they should come to harm. He was sure that he should try and get in touch with the village beyond the lake before the snow came. He needed a horse, but he dared not ask Raoul if he might take Mahruss. There was danger, and Mahruss was more precious than anything else that Raoul owned.

By tea-time everyone was exhausted; they had worried and fretted, hidden alone to mourn; they had worked as never before, bringing in wood, and bringing in water; bringing in milk, and making food for vast numbers. Rooms had been tidied and each family now had its own place to go; they had few comforts but they were alive.

Mark Hunter came over after tea. He spoke to Raoul and they went off to the study and were there for a very long time. Micky bedded the mare and fed her; he fed Mahruss, and comforted Trunca, who always needed more attention than the other two. He checked the cow; she would calve within the week. She looked at him curiously from the door of her stall.

Outside, sheep bleated as the men took hay to them. At this rate there would soon be no more hay. There was little grass on the sodden fields. The cows needed food, too, or they would lose their milk.

Raoul came to join Micky as Mark Hunter rode off on his bay gelding.

'Micky, Mark thinks you and he should set off to-morrow and try to get in touch with the rest of the world somehow; we don't know what has happened to other people; the road on the opposite side of the village has obviously disappeared; we expected at least a helicopter over; but nothing has come. Would you go with Mark? — You can ride Mahruss . . .'

'Hasn't Mark any other riding horse?' Micky asked.

'Mahruss knows you; and you know him. We need help — and we will soon need food. We need fuel for the generators; we need someone to help these people make plans. Yet we are as isolated as if we were in my own country. All the 'phones are dead . . .'

'We'll leave at first light,' Micky said.

It would be a nightmare journey; they had to cross fields; had to find a way over the foothills, and he knew that there were bogs in which a man and a horse could vanish. The weather was likely to worsen.

Djeroua whinnied; Mahruss answered her. Inside the house a dog barked, and Naseem growled deep in his throat. He was not happy at the change in his life; so many people bewildered him.

Raoul quieted the dog, a hand on his shoulder.

'You will need food; and you must watch out for Gareth — find out if he is safe. You had better borrow my warm ski anorak, and take a rucksack. One of the families has one; they brought spare clothes in it. I have seen it about. Ask Sian for food; and hot coffee in a flask. There is a flask somewhere in the kitchen. You will need food for Mahruss; take horse nuts with you; you may well be gone for two or three days. Mark says that he knows a path that should take you over to one of the farms on the other side of the Old Man.'

Micky went indoors to talk to Sian. Angharad was drinking tea. When she had finished she drained the cup and looked hard and long at the pattern in the leaves.

'What do you see?' Micky asked.

Angharad said nothing. She rinsed the cup with milk, filled it again, and handed it to Micky before leaving the room. The sound of her tapping footsteps died away down the long corridor.

Micky took a scone and buttered it, and munched, his thoughts on the journey he was to take: fear nudged him. He was safe here; he loved the horses. And he would be riding Mahruss. One step off the path; one trip against a rock, one careless move and he could have an injured horse, or worse, a dead horse.

Outside, in the yard, the dim lights shone across the cobbles. The generator would soon run out of fuel and everyone would be in the dark. Mark had brought some fuel, but there was not enough to run it for long. Firelight danced in every room; they needed curtains and carpets, chairs and beds; somewhere inside the house a baby was crying.

Angharad needed to be alone. There were so many people round her. She longed for her quiet cottage, her peaceful garden and her bees. She would have told them of her doings, and of the birth of the new foal; she would have sung to them softly, knowing that even though they slept their winter sleep, they were aware of the world outside, and aware of her.

She closed her eyes briefly and saw them dancing above the clover; a bright sun shining, and a world at peace. She opened them again and looked down at the scar of water — at the foaming rush and the angry boil. She went out and walked across the field, among the sheep. They watched her, eyes curious but unafraid.

Angharad walked on, almost to the water's edge. A bunch of flowers, still held in place by a raffia band that clutched the stems loosely, lay on the bank. Winter flowers from her winter garden. Flowers that had lain on the Gipsy's grave.

She turned and walked up the hill, seeing nothing but the grass that had once grown green over the little patch, and from long ago a voice mocked her. It was

74

the voice of a gipsy boy who had looked like Micky; a boy with dark, curly hair, and dark, laughing eyes who had teased her and offered her the chance to be his bride — to take to the road and live with him as the circus people lived. It would have been a very different life. But war came and the gipsy boy joined the men who lay in graves in foreign lands, and her only memory of him had been this long-ago grave of another gipsy boy. She tended it with love, remembering.

Walking on, slowly, she felt an old woman, and very tired. Raoul met her at the edge of the field.

'There is a time for grieving,' he said. 'It passes.'

She looked at him, and smiled.

'I am in my own country,' she said. 'Will you ever return to yours?'

Raoul looked back into the desert — back to the days when he had had a wife and a baby son, and friends about him; and plans to make for his people.

'They would kill me if I went back,' he said. He looked at the Old Man, at the wicked cliff towering into sky that only yesterday had been a gentle slope, earth and rock lying above the escarpment, hiding it from the world below.

'Life changes overnight,' he said.

'You wait nine months for the babe. The child is born, and though you waited and prepared, life has changed, in a second. It is never the same again. Springtime and harvest, birth and dying; they all happen fast and are soon over.'

'Will Micky be safe?' Raoul asked.

Angharad glanced at him. She did not wish to look into the future; the future was better unknown; sometimes it was not possible to live with foreknowledge.

She looked down at the water.

'I see two endings,' she said. 'In one, horse and rider come safely home, and all is well. In the other, a gipsy boy on a wonderful stallion joins Cafell, and the three of them protect the travellers on the hills from danger for ever. They run in front of the wind; they

ride on the wind; and above the hound cry comes the
whinny of a horse and a lad singing; and those who
see them look at them and follow them, and come to
safety and then, as they turn away, see that the three
cast no shadows.'

'What are you telling me?' Raoul aked.

'That what lies in the future must be; I cannot
change it; it is better to wait for the ending, and not to
know.'

'Better never to know?' Raoul asked. 'Better not to
have warning of danger, or to read treason in another
man's eyes?'

'Would it alter anything?' Angharad asked. 'Is not
all written, so that it comes to pass?'

There was a sound of quick hoofbeats. Mark Hunter
came trotting down the hill on his pony. He was a
small man, and rode well; part of the animal, welded
to the saddle, his eyes, as always, bright and searching.

'Gareth's wife is even more distraught,' he said
abruptly. 'Their little collie bitch ran out of the house
and vanished down the hill. She is afraid that Gwenno
will be drowned.'

'Maybe she's gone to look for Gareth,' Angharad
said. "Dogs know much that we don't know.'

Raoul was in the stable, stroking Mahruss. He moved
a lock of shining mane and leaned his head against the
arched neck. The stallion nibbled his ear, lovingly and
gently.

'Take care, my beauty, and come back to me safely,'
Raoul said in his own language, and the stallion bent
his head as if he understood.

Outside in the night the full moon climbed over the
mountain and shone on the stark rock. At almost
every window in the house wakeful eyes watched, looking at the mountain that had destroyed their homes
and their dreams.

Sara thought of her wedding dress, to be worn in a
month's time, now under the water; Sian thought of
the shawl she was making for the little unborn

grandchild in England — her first grandchild. It was almost finished; a shawl for the christening, made night after night with patience and love, as she found the work difficult, her eyes not being young any more. It had to be perfect. Long hours of work, all gone. Hours she could never live again.

The Morrises thought of their little shop — of the hours spent painting and cleaning; arranging the shelves, pricing the goods; the records they had to keep, all buried under the water.

Outside in the barn a little cat brought in her last kitten. She had been living wild behind the shop, fed when they saw her, but often she vanished, hunting on the hills. She had four kittens hidden in the shed, and when the mountain had grumbled first she had run with each one to a place on the high hill, where it was safe.

Now, when men had ceased moving, she brought the kittens to the shelter of the dry hay, to a place where she would find food — where she knew men would help her. Raoul, who could not sleep, came out of the stable and saw her carrying the last kitten. He thought it was a rat, until he heard it mew, and he went to look at her nest. The kits were tiny, their eyes unopened. Going indoors he made bread and milk for the cat. Then he brought it out and stood watching her.

She lived her life among men, yet was so secretive. She owned a world he could never enter; and she could never enter his. She rubbed against his leg, purring, thanking him for food, and he went indoors to lie awake, and think of the long-ago camel trains and the bright sun of the desert sands that he would never see again.

Micky slept; he had nothing to forget and had lost nothing. He had never had anything to lose, not since his grandfather died. Tomorrow he would take the stallion that he adored, and together they would ride and bring help to the villagers.

Tomorrow he would start a new legend; tomorrow he would be a hero. He dreamed that he was a king riding on a horse that galloped among the clouds, his great wings beating — a king among men and a king among horses. He turned over, flinging an arm above his head, and the full moon streamed across the floor, patterning the room with dreamlight.

CHAPTER SEVEN

MORNING was bright, fine and frosty. Mark Hunter waited at the door while Micky and Raoul saddled Mahruss. Micky was dressed in borrowed clothes — Raoul's cashmere jersey, which was warmer and softer than anything he had known before, and his ski anorak, padded with duck down, light as snowflakes.

Mark was equally warmly dressed. They both carried small rucksacks. Mark's wife had been lavish with food, and Sian had prepared as if Micky were going on a fortnight's journey, instead of, as they hoped, being gone perhaps only two days.

They were about to set off when the sound of another horse trotting reached them. Mahruss whinnied, and Mark's pony echoed the sound.

Owen Pritchard came into sight, trotting on an old bay mare. She looked as if she could scarely draw breath, let alone be ridden over the ground they would have to take. Every sign of a road had gone.

'I know these hills; and both of you are strangers to them,' old Owen said. He was as old as the Old Man himself, Micky thought, looking at him. Owen rarely came down to the village or passed the house. He was a grandfather who owned the farm and told the men what to do, keeping himself busy about the place.

'I can ride the two of you into the ground and so can old Nina here,' the old man said, grinning at them.

He had his own teeth still, what was left of them, and his mouth was a fearsome sight when it opened. Grey hair straggled over an almost bald head; but his eyes were dark grey, deep and compelling, and expressed much that his mouth did not.

'We go over the big field, through the gate, and down the bridle path until the river stops us,' Owen said, leading the way through the milling sheep that flocked together, before scattering in front of the horses.

Micky rode after them in a daze of delight. He was riding Mahruss; he was riding to glory, he was riding a dream of a horse, a beauty of a horse, a horse that every man would covet. He looked down at the head, at the sharp pricked ears that moved, listening; Mahruss heard noises that no man could hear.

The stallion knew there was a shivering weasel hiding, almost under his hooves, caught unawares as it was busy eating a rabbit. He knew there was the little cat crouched in the long grass, her eyes on a mousehole, her tail erect, quivering with excitement; he knew that a thrush hid in the bush, waiting till they had gone. He picked his way delicately, treading lightly, following behind Nina and Mark Hunter's chestnut pony, Bracken. Both were mares.

Micky was aware that the stallion moved proudly, every muscle working perfectly, no hint of a falter, whether he walked or trotted, but it was the first time he had had him on his own, without Raoul's watchful eyes. Raoul would be following him in thought, ever present, whatever they did.

'Trust me,' he said to the presence in his mind. 'I would never hurt him.'

He whispered endearing words he would never speak aloud to the horse, and watched the two men in front of him. Old Owen sank into the mare, his body a heap of bones, yet he rode her easily, occasionally straightening as if remembering his own youth.

They reined in at the edge of the field and looked down. Below them water foamed and frothed, throwing debris on to the banks; memories of other people's loves — a broken doll; a toy horse, a piece of wood from a broken chest. Everything that entered the water was pounded and smashed and, as they walked on once more and came to the bridle path, they turned a bend and saw water pouring off the heights, a roaring torrent that would never cease.

The village would not rise again from under the water. Nothing could turn that gushing river away from the rock.

'We are lucky to live high,' old Owen said. 'Above the danger, above the water; we have everything still, and they have nothing.'

They rode in silence.

No one could find words to match those; Mark thought of his wife, safe at home, everything that they had gathered over the years surrounding her, the children safe with her; his beasts all safe, nothing lost. And the people who were sheltering with them, marooned in time, with no knowledge of what lay ahead. Nothing to remind them of the past; the little things, the silly things.

What did he treasure? His father's watch; it would never go again, but when he looked at it, he remembered a happy childhood. His mother's picture, in its silver frame; the pictures of the children when they were babies. Owen thought of the past; of the days when he was strong. He straightened his back. He was riding out for help as a young man rode. He was not finished or useless; there was life in the old man yet. He turned his head and saw Micky riding, his eyes dreaming, a dark boy on a horse that was beautiful beyond poetry. Kings rode such horses; not gipsy boys. And the man who owned it, he walked like a king and might once have been a king in another land far away; a silent man without much to say for himself, a man who had generously thrown open his home when it was needed; a man who treasured his horses beyond his life, and yet let a lad from nowhere take his greatest possession, and ride into danger.

For there would be danger. The slopes were steep and slippery. They had to cross Merlin's Bog, and the heavens alone knew what had happened there in recent days with so much rain. Deep and dark and peaty, treacherous and wicked, men had died in the bog through the centuries. These two would never manage alone; Owen, looking at the clouds building above the Old Man, wondered if any of them would come home. There might be another Gipsy's grave for Angharad to tend.

Angharad.

He had known her all his life; remembered her as a girl, beautiful beyond all the village girls, with blue eyes, and bright hair that lay thick on her shoulders or was bound with blue ribbons. He had never seen her wear any colour but blue. The blue of the skies. Once he had written poems to her; but he had never sent them. Once he had watched her wistfully, but he had never spoken and the gipsy boy had come and stolen her from him; the gipsy boy died and lay under a foreign sun, but by then Owen was married and his wife had two babies.

And now those babies were grown men, working with the sheep, with babes of their own.

Over the Old Man the shaggy clouds thickened. A few flakes of snow brushed Micky's cheek. They were riding above the river; among the memories of the village tossed upon the banks. A great tree swirled in midstream, caught by a rock that held it, and then it freed itself and surged on. A dead hen floated by.

Mahruss paused in his stride, his ears pricked forwards. Something was hidden in a bush, and as he turned his head, Owen whistled and out of the bushes came a small black-and-white bitch, her ears pricked high, her head held on one side, one paw raised. She trotted ahead of them, and turned again, as if asking them to follow.

'It's Gareth's little bitch,' Mark Hunter said. 'I wonder if she knows where he is?'

They forgot the shaggy clouds. The bitch turned up the hill, nose down, questing, following a trail that no man could see.

'She's tracking,' Owen said. 'And she isn't tracking rabbit. There are no beasts on this hill; I do not know why; there is a story that Cafell has hunted them all to extinction. We are in his territory. Soon we will hear him whining.'

The little bitch moved purposefully up the hill, away from the water. She paused often to make sure the men were following, and soon all three were convinced they were on Gareth's trail.

'Time to rest the horses,' Owen said. He whistled the bitch and she came. But she lay poised, ready to move again, watching as the men dismounted, taking flasks from their bags and pouring coffee. The horses were tethered to the trees, grazing the ground at their hooves.

Owen looked up at the sky.

'We are in for trouble,' he said. 'The wind has changed; tonight snow will come and Cafell will cry; my family always calls him the Hound of Darkness. You never see him when it is light. But when dusk comes, he runs down the hill, dark and big and as beautiful as he was when Arthur was king; and he guides the traveller to safety. Please God he will come to us.'

'Does he always come?' Micky asked, not believing in the ghost dog.

'Not always. Some men are beyond help; sometimes it is better there should be no help. Who can tell? Maybe as we have the little bitch to guide us, we will not need Cafell. Maybe he does not exist; only an old man's story, told by the fire at night. I have never seen Cafell. Nor have I met any man who has; but there are many stories, told in the firelight, told through the ages.'

They ate a little food and drank the hot coffee; and then it was time to ride. The litle bitch ran ahead of them, streaking up the hill to the trail she had left, and on, nose down, but slowly, so that the horses could keep pace with her.

'I hope she knows what she's doing,' Mark said, wondering if they were wise to follow. They were on a trail now, a gravelly shingle that was part of an old river bed, climbing high.

'We're making for Ty Croes,' Owen said. 'It's a funny way to go, but a man in a hurry might try to reach it this way. It's on the other side of the hill. Not far now.'

They topped the hill and looked down. The old house lay hugging the ground, its slate roof mossed and sagging, dipped at one end. Great shaggy clouds hung about them now, and snow was beginning to fall. The soft wet flakes clung to clothing and to the horses' manes.

The bitch had vanished. They heard her voice, sudden and high, raised in excited greeting. She barked, and other barks echoed round her as the farm dogs joined in.

'Gareth is safe,' Owen said, and urged his mare to trot. She rattled along, every movement ungainly, while behind came Mark's neat pony, and then Mahruss, stepping out nobly. Micky's quick eyes looked around the farmyard at the pecking hens — far too many for the space. He took in the massed sheep beyond the fence, packed so tightly they could barely move, the barns, where cows were housed; and he knew that beasts had found shelter.

There were soft Welsh voices inside, as Owen, having tied his horse, went indoors. Mark and Micky followed, more slowly, to find the old kitchen filled with people. They sat on chairs and on the floor, while Gareth lay on his back on an old settle, his face white, his arm and leg bandaged.

'I fell,' Gareth said. 'I've hurt my ankle.'

Eileen Jones was pouring tea, dark and strong, and full of sugar. She had come from Scotland long ago on a holiday and stayed and married. Her accent was still soft with the gentle burr of Inverness.

'Have you seen what has happened?' Owen asked. The village was invisible from here.

'I saw, yesterday,' a voice said from the shadows of the old dresser. Firelight gleamed on willow-pattern plates. The soft glow of an oil lamp cast shadows everywhere. It was impossible to see how many people there were. A solemn, small boy played with his bricks in the middle of the hearth rug, too young to be aware of sorrow.

'What will we do?' a forlorn voice asked from the darkness.

Nobody answered.

'We are trying to get to one of the farms that still has a 'phone working,' Mark said. 'We need food, clothes, and bedding; and fuel for the generators.'

'They will have to bring a helicopter,' another voice said. 'The road at the bottom is also under water; I can see the roofs of cars.'

'Were there people in the cars?'

Gareth shook his head.

'That was how I was hurt. I was bringing them up here, and I slipped on the wet mud and crashed into a tree; I've sprained my ankle and torn a tendon in my wrist. Luckily one of the cars was driven by a doctor.'

'Do any of you need help?' a man asked. He came forward, a small man with dark eyes, his once neat suit crumpled. 'I have my medical bag.'

'Everyone was well when we left,' Mark said.

Micky had gone to the door to look at the horses. Outside was darker than night and snow was falling. Enormous flakes lay on the horses' saddles and clung to hair and clothing, masking the cobbled ground.

'It's snowing hard,' he said, turning back into the kitchen.

'Then we need to bring in wood and water,' the farmer said, heaving himself from his corner. He was a fat man, his clothes hugging him tightly, brown eyes always laughing, grey hair curly and thick. His wife nodded.

'The horses are in the barn. We have hay enough for a few days; they can feed on calf nuts. We must bring wood in and keep the yard clear. The chickens must be put in the end barn; let's hope they don't all fight. There are two cocks. They need caging, or there will be trouble.'

Within moments everyone was busy; some taking hay to the cattle; some taking hay to the sheep, huddled and miserable against the wall; the dogs ran everywhere, getting underfoot, but the little collie bitch was with her master, her nose in his hand.

'If only we could tell Megan that Gareth is safe,' Micky said, as he unsaddled Mahruss and put him, away from the the two mares, in one of the old stalls in the barn. He spread straw thickly under the horse. There was a peat floor in the barn, thickly covered for all the animals.

Boys carried in wood. The place was so small it seemed impossible that everyone would fit in, but somehow they all did. Eileen had managed, with the women helping her, to instil an air of holiday, to laugh at difficulties. They had brewed gallons of tea and coffee, and had made a great baking of bread and buns, Bara Brith and scones. There was an enormous jam-making pan filled with thick vegetable soup, and great, crusty lumps of wholemeal bread thick with goat butter, and hunks of goat cheese. The kitchen was the only room with a fire, and as no one had bedding, the fire was to be kept in all night. People would have to sleep where they could.

There was water from the well; they had never depended on piped water here. Micky helped fill buckets for the animals, aware that the snow was lying thickly, and that they would soon be unable to move away from the cottage. Outside, the Old Man had disappeared, totally hidden in thick cloud that covered him from head to foot.

Inside, someone brought out a mouth-organ and began to play. Micky caught the tune and whistled it, and soon everyone was singing. There was nothing else to do; they had mourned for hours; and now they were grateful for life, even if they did not know what the future held. They were bound by shared disaster. They were back in the Middle Ages; there was no electricity here, either; maybe a pylon was down under the flood, maybe worse; or the substation had been hit by boulders under water. They had no radio, as the only one in the house had died, needing another battery. One of the children began to cry and his mother hushed him.

'I want light,' he sobbed. 'Switch on the light. I don't like the shadows. Cafell is in the shadows.'

'Listen,' Micky said suddenly. 'I remember a poem my mother used to say about light. It's lovely. It's about a light like this, an oil light: soft light, not hard, electric light. Light for dreams, light to sing by, light to sit by, light to court by. My mother used to light the lamp in our cottage; it was a dark, dreadful, little cottage, the walls damp, the paper peeling off them, and she and my dad hated it; to us, it was home, especially when the fire was lit and we were warm, and we had bread and soup, like you have now. Shall I tell it to you?'

He could just see the child in the shadows; a small solemn face, brown curly hair, cheeks tearstained and dirty. The child nodded.

'My mother called it the Grace for Light. She came from Ireland; we lived in Liverpool, that's a long way from here — a big, dirty city; no green fields, and no trees to climb. It went like this:

> "When we were little childer we had a quare wee house,
> Away up in the heather by the head o' Brabla burn;
> The hares we'd see them scootin', and we'd hear the crowin' grouse,
> And when we'd all be in at night ye'd not get room to turn.

*The youngest two she'd put to bed, their faces to
  the wall,*
*And the lave of us could sit aroun', just anywhere
  we might;*
Herself 'ud take the rush-dip and light it for us all,
*'An' God be thanked,' she would say, — 'now, we
  have a light.'*

*Then we be quiet to laughin' and pushin' on the
  floor,*
*An' think of One who called to us to come and be
  forgiven;*
*Himself 'ud put his pipe down, an' say the good
  word more,*
*'May the Lamb o' God lead us all to the Light of
  Heaven!'*

*There's a wheen things that used to be an' now has
  had their day,*
*The nine Glens of Antrim can show ye many a
  sight;*
*But not the quare wee house where we lived up
  Brabla 'way,*
*Nor a child in all the nine Glens that knows the
  Grace for Light." '*

His voice ended; it had taken on his mother's accent
— the soft Irish lilt he had almost forgotten. He had
been as small as the wee one there, curled safe on his
mother's lap, leaning against her, listening to her. And
sometimes she had sung softly to him, and he had felt
safe and at peace.

The child was asleep. Everyone was busy with their
own thoughts, for here they were, in a room as small
as that room in the little Irish cottage. Sitting where
they could, they were so crowded there was barely
space to move.

Outside, the cattle lowed. Mahruss whinnied and the
mares answered. Sheep bleated.

Mark looked out of the window. Snow was falling thick and fast, whirling on the wind. Outside, night had come, fully an hour early. Snow lay on the ground and built against the window. They were in for a rough time.

'We can't go on tomorrow; we would never find our way anywhere, and we might end up dead,' Mark said softly. Owen, behind them, looked into the darkness beyond the window.

'We can only pray,' he said.

Behind them a soft voice began to tell the children of the fairy lady of Llyn Fan Fach, who came from the lake with her beautiful cattle and married a mortal man. She would stay with him only if he never struck her. They lived very happily until one fine day a hornet came and flew around her, and her husband, trying to kill the hornet, struck her on the cheek. That night she vanished and all the beasts with her except a new, white calf. She left her three sons, and they became great healers.

'I am one of her descendants,' the doctor said from the darkness. He laughed, and no one knew if he were speaking the truth.

'And Angharad is another,' Owen said. 'The lady's descendants are sometimes blue-eyed, fair-haired and beautiful, and when Angharad was young there wasn't a girl in miles to touch her. There's beautiful, she was.' His voice was wistful, and Micky thought of Angharad, whose eyes were wise, and who seemed to him very old, and he suddenly saw her as she once had been and knew that Owen spoke the truth.

Micky kicked off his shoes, and rolled Raoul's anorak up inside his pack, and went to sleep, to dream of riding Mahruss on the wind, flying along a ridge, while a great river surged below. He rode over a meadow and he rode over the sands; and he reined in where the sea met the land. He spoke to the stallion and together they swam into the waves. It was deep green beneath the sea. A black hound watched them, waving his stern in greeting.

The light grew whiter — so blinding that it hurt.

Mark woke. He was lying beneath the window, and the day had come; day dawning in a sea of snow that rose half way up the window, hiding the yard. He had never seen so much snow in his life.

CHAPTER EIGHT

RAOUL woke early and went downstairs to stare out into a world that had changed overnight. He had never seen snow before; the last year there had been a little sleet, but nothing more. Snow lay against the windows; hiding the sills. Snow covered the yard. A bird had walked across, marking it with spidery tracks.

Snow hid the fields; the sheep were packed, backs huddled against the walls, bleating. The back door to the yard would not open, and he thrust his weight against it uselessly.

'We will have to get the men up, and the women will have to prepare hot food. We must clear the snow in the yard, and see to the sheep,' Angharad said, coming into the kitchen. She looked out at the Old Man, who brooded in the distance, his shape masked. He was stern and tall and beautiful, glistening in the morning sun, but she knew that when the snows melted, the river that raged now would be a torrent such as none of them had ever seen. It could not rise here, but any hope of salvaging anything at all from under those waters was gone for ever.

The front door opened into a garden that had ceased to exist. The children were excited; nothing could mar their spirits for long and this was all new, all different. They could toboggan down the slope in the field, and build snowmen. Their voices sounded on the air as they raced around, the adults too busy to check them.

The women helped Sian prepare breakfast: porridge, eggs, and rounds of toast, which the men ate between working, slipping in, eating fast and returning to work again. They were clearing a track across the yard to the stables, clearing snow from the back door, clearing paths to barn and byre and to the sheep field.

They were over the wall in the sheep field, plunging deep, and found two lambs, buried in snow beside mothers that bleated helplessly and forlornly. The sheep needed both warmth and feeding. The ewes had no milk for their lambs. Angharad took them into an empty stall in the stables and bedded them on hay. Feeding was not easy for there were no feeding bottles. She filled an orange-squash bottle with warm milk, and one of the farmers fitted it with a cork and a piece of tubing, and they fed the lambs with that; it was necessary to be careful, or the tiny creatures would choke.

The ewes were given milk in buckets and extra hay; maybe with that they would make their own milk.

Raoul watched the feeding, and took one of the lambs. He held it up to Djeroua.

'You have milk and to spare, my beauty,' he said to the mare. 'Let the little ones feed.' He held the lamb to the mare's udder and it began to suck.

Naseem watched with interest. The big German Shepherd dog was now never far from his master; he slept by Raoul's bed and walked with him wherever he went. Raoul let the lamb feed for a few minutes, and took it back to its mother, who nuzzled it close as she lay in the straw. The baby slept.

Raoul lifted the second lamb. Djeroua watched quietly. Raoul was all her life, and she trusted him completely. He tended and fed her and cared for her and her foal, and she was gentle and kind and understood well that this young creature needed her milk, too. Angharad watched, marvelling at the patient hands that were so large and yet so soft in touch, and the care with which the lambs were carried. Raoul looked so fierce at times, yet with the beasts was gentler than any man she had ever met.

'We live with our horses in my country,' Raoul said. 'The highest honour in our land is to care for a horse.

There is no creature like it; Mahruss is more precious to me than anything else in the world.' He walked over to the stable door. Behind him a lamb bleated softly and the mother baa'd in answer. The foal sneezed, and Djeroua rustled in the straw as she moved towards her haynet. Beyond him the world stretched endlessly white, every landmark gone, every house hidden; only plumes of smoke round the bare chimney stacks showed that there was life on the other farms.

'If they were caught in the snow . . .' Raoul began, his eyes following the ground as if he could pick out Micky, Mark, and Owen, and their horses as they rode.

'We can only pray,' Angharad said, watching the children laughing as if nothing had changed in their lives, as they dodged the snowballs. 'We must warn them not to wander. The drifts are deep.'

'It is very beautiful,' Raoul said, looking at the snow-laden trees, at the glitter on the ground, and at the clear blue sky from which a cold sun shone, barely warming the ground. Frost had hardened the snow. Frost rimed the window panes.

The children stood and watched their breath plume on the air.

'I'm smoking,' one of the boys called and stood puffing plumes from his mouth, amusing himself immensely.

Raoul fed the mare and groomed her; he watched the foal feed; he lifted the lambs again so that each could have more milk; he cleaned the stable, sweeping the straw into a corner and then into the barrow. The yard was now marked with hundreds of footprints and the snow was dirty and mired with mud. One of the men passed him, carrying a sack laden with newly cut logs. Sian called to him to stop work and come and feed; a man needed food.

He went indoors and paced restlessly, looking out at the Old Man, thinking of Micky with Mahruss, out there somewhere, perhaps buried under the snow.

Angharad collected the women together to make lists of all the food in the house. They had milk enough for days, and could live on it if need be. They could melt the snow for water, and the children were set to filling pails of snow and bringing them into the warm kitchen; clean snow from the fields. The men were clearing the biggest barn and lining the floor with straw, and bringing in the sheep.

Clouds were building again on the Old Man and the wind was whining.

'Cafell is calling,' one of the children said.

'Cafell is guarding us,' Angharad said.

Gareth's pretty wife had come to join them, hoping for early news. She was sitting by the fire, her thoughts on her husband. She could settle to nothing. Angharad gave her the potatoes to peel, knowing she needed occupation. There was nothing anyone could do for her. Sian found herself wondering if Raoul cared more about the possible loss of his stallion than about Micky. Old Owen should not have gone with them; an old man on an old horse in this wild weather . . .

The wind was whining more loudly, whipping the snow so that it blew off the drifts, piling up against the house again. The clouds that swirled over the Old Man thickened and deepened and grew until the day was night-dark, and fresh snowflakes were drifting on the wind. The children came in, frightened.

The animals were as safe as was possible. Raoul put out hay for the mare and the sheep, and the cow in the end byre; she might calve soon and her owner wanted to spend his time with her, but it was not safe. They might not be able to get across the yard. Which was more valuable, the life of a man or the life of a beast? And it was bitterly cold in the stables. Djeroua was rugged, and the straw deep at her feet, and Raoul had taken a mohair lap rug and fastened it on the foal. Angharad had stitched strings to tie it. They had to make do, and invent, all the time.

94

By mid-afternoon no one could go outside. The dogs were given a deep bed of peat to use for their own needs in the outhouse that led off Micky's little room. Outside had vanished in the swirling snow. It was impossible to see beyond the windows. No one had seen snow like this before. Raoul, pacing restlessly from end to end of his study, watched the windows vanish. He drew the curtains, but he could not draw curtains on his thoughts. If Mark and Micky and Owen were caught outside in this they would never return.

Mahruss would lie dead; and his dreams would go with the stallion, because there would be no more foals from him. If only Trunca's foal were a colt foal, to grow into a stallion as good as Mahruss . . .

Angharad had collected everyone together in the big kitchen which was the warmest room in the house. The beat of the generator sounded from the outhouse. It was a background to all their thoughts and all their voices, a protection against darkness, but it would not run for ever. Oil lamps were ready to light; Sian had found a cache of candles stored by someone long before Raoul came, some eaten by mice, but most of them intact, right at the back of the cupboard under the sink.

Angharad began to sing and soon everyone joined in. Raoul listened, but he needed to be alone. No one could share his worries; he had lost his land and he had lost his wife; he had lost his son; how could he make these people, who had each other still and were in their own country, understand that he had only his horses as his sole reason for living. If Mahruss died . . .

It was necessary to plan. He glanced along the shelves and took down one of the many books that he found a help in this strange country. He knew how to keep horses in his own land; how to care for horses in his own climate, how to feed his horses on the foods available. Here, he was learning all the time.

He had had to drain his land to make it fit for the horses. The drains would be broken by the snow; he would need to start work again. The soil was heavy and would be sodden and it would be weeks before he could let the horses run free. He had never known such winters before; winter that froze the ground, killing the grass and freezing the water; winter that brought snow to cover the land.

He planned to re-sow the meadows with good grass; he would need to find men to help him and maybe those who were here would be able to do that. He did not like to ask, but if he were to earn enough to keep him and his horses and this house in this very expensive country, then it would be to their benefit to ensure that all was well. He could not imagine where the families would go if they did not stay here. There was nowhere in the village to build now; the Old Man had ensured, overnight, that everything had gone. But they were lucky to be alive.

His thoughts went round and round in his head, in his own language, so that when Angharad came in with tea and freshly baked scones, and spoke to him in English, the words did not make sense.

'You must eat,' she said again. 'Come and join us. It is better not to be alone at such times. They will have found shelter.'

'Do you believe that?' Raoul asked, thinking with difficulty in English. 'How can they be safe?'

'I feel it,' Angharad said. 'Once, I might have read the future; now, I prefer not to know; but I am sure they are safe. The snow will go; and the world will carry on as before; and we will be rescued.'

Raoul sipped the hot, sweet tea, and broke off a piece of buttered scone.

'Flood and fire; hurricane and typhoon; avalanche and earthquake. You would think men had enough to do fighting nature, without the need to fight one another.' He looked into the fire; little flames danced and died; a tiny cave of wood shone bright at the back of the hearth and in it a flame flickered, dragonlike, and flashed and brightened. Wood cracked as fresh twigs caught fire.

'I am planning for the future,' Raoul said. 'Maybe I am only dreaming, but it helps.'

'What are you planning?' Angharad sat herself in the big, leather arm chair, and was lost, a tiny woman, little of her showing but her bright eyes which watched him, knowing he needed distraction.

'Hay,' Raoul said, and laughed. 'I have to learn how to feed horses in this country, and there are more types of hay than most people realize.'

Angharad nodded.

'Meadow hay and clover hay; sainfoin hay and the best of them all, lucerne hay. My father had horses, and he grew lucerne and clover; he would only give them the best. He would sniff it and test it with his fingers; it must never be musty; it must never be clammy; it must be dry and rattly and feel right when it's held. Hay must be cut at the right time; not too soon and not too late. There's an art in it, as in all farming.'

'Would you like to stay here?' Raoul asked. 'There is far too much room in this house for one man and a boy, and Micky will not stay for ever.'

'Micky has springs in his heels and may take off at any time,' Angharad said, 'but he also has horses in his blood and I doubt if he will ever find such horses again. And I — we will see when the snow goes.'

Darkness had come early. Outside, the snow had once more covered the yard thickly, but the wind had eased, and the blizzard was over. The men began to clear a path, to reach the stock, take hay, and check the ewes, so that they could remove those about to lamb. There were problems now about space. If too many lambs were born, there was no indoor place left to put them. Every corner was occupied.

Djeroua whinnied when Raoul opened the stable door; the foal bucked and greeted him, her small world centering on this one place, and on these people. The ewes both had milk now, and their lambs were feeding. They looked up at the men who came into the shadowy buildings.

The children indoors were quarrelsome, too long together. They were put to bed, and the adults settled to a late meal. Islanded in time, they were flung out of reality. Reality had been a home of their own and familiar places; a desk in the schoolroom, a bed of one's own; the pattern of the wallpaper, of the curtains, of carpets, of bed covers, as familiar as the sight of one's own face in the mirror every morning.

Reality had been a familiar routine; alarm clock and rising, dressing, shaving for the men, which still continued for some, but with borrowed razors. Two had decided to grow beards, so that they were unfamiliar to their own families. Reality was eating breakfast in one's own place, in one's own home; the drive to work, or the bicycle ride, or the walk along a road, knowing every corner; the pillar box let into the wall; the 'phone kiosk on the curve of the lane; the thirty mile-an-hour sign that stood just before the school entrance, and the sign pointing to the school itself.

Reality was familiar clothes, and lacing up shoes, and fetching out the box of cleaning equipment; taking the vacuum cleaner around the house, washing and ironing, baking and sewing, watching the clock tick away the minutes, telling of a child coming home for tea, a man coming in for supper. Reality was the weekend, and families visiting and talking on the corner, and the vital news of birth and death: a calf born to the farmer up the lane; a baby born to Mair in the end house; a girl about to marry; an old man to be buried; the shop where food was bought and stamps were sold, and people met to chat and laugh.

Reality was running up the hillside with a dog at heel; fishing in the little stream, and bringing home a trout for tea; meeting in the Lion at night, the men laughing and talking and playing darts; the new juke box that the younger people loved and the old men hated; the veterinary surgeon coming in every week to hold his surgery; the doctor's surgery at the end of the lane, open only in the afternoons. The building had once been a shop.

Reality was the way your family fed; and the way your family thought; and the closeness together at night.

All that had gone. Even the world they knew had gone now, buried under the snow the few familiar landmarks; and, above them all, towering in his grandeur — fierce and unpredictable — with who knew what further dangers in store for them, was the Old Man. In his new shape, he was as strange as the once familiar street — now the bed for a raging river that tossed tree trunks as if they were small sticks, and flung foam high in the air, threatening death to anyone that stood on its banks.

That night more snow fell, and families lay awake, fearing further disaster. Angharad, wakeful, wondered what had happened to the rest of the world; wondered if anyone knew what had happened to the village. She planned how best to make use of the food they had, as there was no way now that they could get help even from the other farms on the little hill. They were completely cut off until the thaw came.

Raoul could not sleep at all. He sat in his library, keeping the fire alive with small offerings of wood, aware that fuel could be a problem soon, as they needed to gather so much with so many families in the house.

He thought of Djeroua's foal. He had promised Micky that he would write out a birth certificate for her, as they were once written in his own country, and as they had been written in past times in England.

He would spend the night lettering it and drawing tiny foals all around the edge. Sleep would never come.

He began to write. By three in the morning his work was completed and he was tired enough to go to bed. He slept on the divan in his study. Others slept in his

99

bedroom now. He read the certificate carefully. He would frame it and put it over Micky's bed as a surprise for the lad when he came home, bringing Mahruss with him. The lettering was even and beautiful; tiny foals played all around the edge of the paper, slender, elegant, with softly-falling manes and tails that were like those on a child's rocking horse. A promise of a mane when the foal was grown. He loved the little mane on Djeroua's foal — Rhiannon, goddess of horses, born in a strange land and taking the name of a Welsh goddess.

He read the deed again.

'God.

Enoch.

In the name of the most merciful God, the Lord of all creatures, peace and prayers be with our Lord Mahomet and his family and his followers, until the day of Judgement, and peace be with all those who read this writing and understand its meaning.

The present deed relates to a creamy brown filly, with two white feet and a star on its forehead, of the true breed of Arab horses, resembling those horses of whom the Prophet said "True riches are a noble and pure breed of horses," and of which God said "The warhorses, those which plunge into battle in the morning."

And God spoke the truth in his incomparable books.

This horse was bred by Raoul, who was once a Sheikh in his land and now lives in exile far from his home among strangers.

Her sire Mahruss is of excellent stock from his own homeland; born of the true Breed. Her dam, Djeroua, is of beauty beyond compare.

According to what we attest here, O Sheikhs of Wisdom and Possessors of Horses, this filly is even more noble than her sire and her dam. And this we attest according to our best knowledge by this valid and perfect deed.

We also attest that this filly is named Rhiannon, in honour of Wales, the country in which she first saw the light of day.

Thanks be to God, the Lord of All Creatures.'

He left the deed on the table, and, when he came in, very early, found Angharad looking at it. She had come in to the library to clean out the fireplace.

'I have never seen anything like it,' she said.

'I made it for Micky. It is a copy of a deed written in 1808, for a long-ago horse, and that in turn was a copy of all the deeds written for all our horses,' Raoul said.

'Were you a sheikh?' Angharad asked.

'I was a king,' Raoul said. He looked out at the snow-blanketed fields and shivered. 'Another man rules in my country now, and brings great sorrow. But I can never go back. Nothing will ever be the same again in my land.'

'Nor here,' Angharad said. 'I would be grateful to you if I can stay. I would hate to leave the valley. My people have always lived here.'

'There will always be room in my house for you,' Raoul said.

He stood beside her, looking up at the Old Man. The mountain was innocent today, white under a blue sky, total perfection. Snow hid the wicked crags and the slopes that had shed earth and trees and buried the village.

The sound of water was almost as loud as the thumping generator.

'We have very little fuel left,' Raoul said.

They went out to battle with the snow in the yard; to struggle with food and water for the animals; to clean out soiled bedding and to bring in new. There was no more time for remembrance; no time for grief.

Only the need to survive — to survive until their small world was joined once more to the world outside and they could find a new way to live.

Raoul opened the stable door and Djeroua whinnied. Rhiannon bounced towards him, so perfect that he caught his breath. Sunlight drifted into the stable.

Here, life was normal; no matter where in the world, where there was a horse there was a stable; where there was a foal there was joy.

Outside, in the yard, Angharad was singing softly.

'Morning has broken, like the first morning.
Blackbird has spoken, like the first bird.'

She went indoors; the words died away on the wind. The snow lay on the fields, unmarked, glistening, and Raoul felt that it symbolized their present situation, hidden from reality, with unknown dangers beneath the deceptive safety.

CHAPTER NINE

THE snow fell without ceasing. The world outside was gone, hidden in a swirl of white. It was a struggle to tend the animals; it was a fight to get to the stables, digging a path through endless drifts that blew against the stable doors, that covered the sheep, that prevented anyone from coming near any of them.

No one could remember snow like this.

It was necessary to ration food; to melt snow for water; to use milk for cooking. There was no way of sending out the milk to the tankers. The cows had to be milked.

They might have been in another world, in another time. Raoul's generator died; the house was a dark cave at night that frightened the children; they had to be careful with oil and paraffin for the lamps; they had to husband the torches. They went to bed at dusk and rose when it was light. They had to be careful with the fires; everyone brought their bedding down to the kitchen and slept on the floor; the rest of the house was icy.

Ten miles away, Micky, Mark and Owen were fighting the same battle. Mahruss and the other two horses were across the yard. The stables faced into the snow; snow built up against them every night. Micky shovelled snow in his sleep; he would have liked to sleep near the stallion; he was worried sick about him in spite of having borrowed rugs for him. He wondered wearily about Djeroua and her foal; would they survive this cold? Would Raoul and the people with him have enough food, enough bedding, enough fuel for the generator; enough warmth?

Snow fell nightly for a week.

Then came a day of brilliant sunshine, the sky blue, the fields white, dazzling the eyes. Gareth, looking from the window, thought of the snow melting; of the water that would swirl off the mountain. They were safe here; and his wife was safe; but any houses lower down the hill might well be swamped and follow the village into eternity.

There would never be another village in the valley.

'It's going to be bad,' old Owen said, looking up at the peaks. He had never seen so much snow, and he was almost eighty.

The buzz of a helicopter startled all of them. They ran outside into the yard; a tiny group of people isolated by weather, isolated by disaster. The helicopter flew low, dropping five sacks as it passed. A man leaned out of it, as they turned, and appeared to be counting; they moved apart so he could see how many there were. He waved, and everyone watched as the tiny link with reality disappeared into the distance.

The sacks lay in deep snow beyond the wall.

'Watch for drifts,' old Owen said, but too late, as Micky vanished up to his neck. They hauled him out, and looked again for the sacks. It was necessary once more to dig, and dig fast, as the sky was darkening and the ominous storm clouds were building again on the peaks.

It took three hours to reach their trophies, and another hour to drag them back into the farmhouse.

There were tins of every description, and there was a roar of laughter as they took out twenty tins of evaporated milk. Every utensil in the place was full of milk. Most of it had been poured away. The cows couldn't be left unmilked.

One sack contained sleeping-bags, which were very welcome; they had not nearly enough blankets.

There was chocolate for the children; jellies and bread mixes; packets of custard, and instant puddings. Everything light and useful had been crammed inside.

They fed well and settled down early, and Micky watched the snow blot out the sky. Sometime during the night the snow turned to rain. He heard it whisper against the windows; and above the noise heard the sound of the wind keening round the house

'Cafell is hunting,' a voice said in the darkness.

By morning, the snow was beginning to thaw. The steady persistent drip sounded endlessly in their ears. They had work to do and fought against the weather, with aching hands and aching arms, and legs that were sore from ploughing through deep snow. It was time to rescue the animals; time to find the buried sheep; time to count the losses, and the losses were going to be high.

The helicopter was able to land three days later. Two men came over to count heads: to find out how many had survived from the village; Micky was able to tell them about Raoul, and the number of families he had with him. They had not yet made contact; the weather had been too bad, but today it would be possible; the wind had died away and the air was still and there would be a chance to see if they could land in the fields. They would take food and fuel for the generator, as well as a doctor, and food for the animals.

The rescue teams had been busy all over the country. There was disaster everywhere; gales and floods and snow had played havoc with communications. Cars were marooned on every high pass; Shap was closed and the Woodhead road near Sheffield, too. It was impossible to travel to and from Scotland; it was impossible to move from east to west, or north to south except by helicopter. Even the airports were closed.

Mark, Micky and Owen could go back as soon as the weather eased. Rescue was in sight. There would be food and bedding, and those who wished would be taken to friends or relatives; help would be given with starting life again. The government knew what had happened to the village; they had declared it a disaster area. Only the weather had prevented help from coming before.

Two days later the three set out again. Most of the snow had gone and the lanes were clear, but the bridle paths were slippery and it was necessary to tread carefully. Micky had terrifying visions of Mahruss slipping and breaking a leg; they need never have gone on this journey. But they hadn't known what was happening; they had had to try.

The day was surprisingly warm, and before they had travelled four miles mist began to rise on the hills. Mist curled around them, tendrils of it smoking above them; mist blotted out the sky; mist blotted out the landmarks.

'Nothing for it but to stop,' old Owen said. 'We could plunge from here to hell in this if we got lost. We've not even Gareth's dog to guide us this time.'

The dog had stayed behind.

The mist grew thicker, but just before dark a small wind began to whisper in the trees. It was an icy wind, a bitter wind, with frost in its teeth. It was a whining wind, and it moaned above them and around them. The horses were uneasy. Mahruss reared high and threw Micky into the heather just as they started, but Micky kept hold of the reins and remounted as soon as the breath was back inside him.

'We can't rest, or we'll freeze,' Mark said.

There was fear in his voice. It was insane to go on, but they had no choice. Owen thought sadly that it was a chilly way for an old man to die; he had never expected to die this way, but death lay before them, one way or another: death on the hills through slipping on the frosty ground. Even if they lay with the horses, and huddled together, this frost was a devil frost with nightmare fingers that would freeze them to death.

It was better to get down and walk beside the horses and lead them; to slip from one place to another, but to keep legs moving; to ride was to freeze, as they couldn't move fast.

There was a thin sliver of moon, a tiny arc riding high, and beyond the moon was the dark night sky and more stars than Micky had ever seen in his life before. It was a bitterly cold night. The mist cleared, and returned wreathing around them.

'We were fools to start,' Mark said. No one answered. It had seemed sensible enough at the time, and the distance was not great; but the mist made movement almost impossible, and it was equally impossible to do more then tread warily, praying they were on the right path, praying that they did not slip and fall to their deaths, praying that the horses did not break their legs.

'I saw a movement,' Mark said, looking ahead into a darkness so unbelievably dense that it seemed to be solid rock.

The mist cleared, the moonlight shivered, and a great dog moved in the shadows and came towards them. He was dark as the night, and large as a wolf-hound, and his eyes glittered, reflecting the stars. He paused, tail moving, one paw raised, looking at them, and then, with a soft whimper, loped along the path in front of them, and paused again. The last trail of mist was ahead of him, and seemed to move away from him as he trotted on.

'He's off the path,' Owen said. 'I'm sure it goes straight, here.'

He tried to move on, but the dog loped back and stood in front of him. His horse stood still.

'It wants us to follow,' Micky said. He whistled. 'Here, lad.'

The dog looked at him, and turned away. This time they followed, and as they turned the angle of the path, Owen reined in his horse and stared. The ground had slipped away; had they gone straight on they would have plunged over a little slope and landed on rocks far beneath.

The dog led them through the darkness.

Their breath plumed above them, and breath feathered from the horses' lips, but there was no breath from the dog.

He paused often to allow them to catch up. In spite of the darkness he was always clearly visible.

The path he led them was an odd path, twisting and turning, not always following a beaten trail. Once they moved through dead bracken on a hillside, once along a gravelly, dry, river bed; none of it was familiar to Owen.

Once Mahruss slipped, his hoof sliding, and Micky caught his breath, praying harder than ever that the horse might not be harmed. He felt the leg, but there was no sign of injury and the stallion plodded on. They were all sleepwalking, all in a dream, all colder than they had ever been in their lives, all removed from reality in a world that had been reduced to glitter and dark, reduced to the soft clip-clop of the horses' shoes when they came on to stone, and the dark shape of the hound that led them.

There were traces still of snow. The sound of rushing water and the high whine of the wind accompanied them all the time.

Micky had forgotten warmth; he had forgotten comfort; he had forgotten ease. He was aware of his frozen face as never before; his nose and his eyes and his lips ached; his chest ached; his legs ached. Old Owen was wondering if he would ever reach his home, would ever last the night, would ever see the dawn; and his old horse was failing.

Dawn came at last. They were still moving slowly, walking gently, following the dog that paused, and paused again; that came back to herd them, to make sure that they kept together. It seemed to have led them on an endless mazy path, but when the day's first light flickered on the hills, they saw the Old Man, and they saw the valley where the torrent raced unchecked, three times as deep as before, spilling over the fields below them. If they had followed the path that Owen knew they would have been trapped by the floods.

Owen knew those floods, flashing down from the hills, a great bore of water that took everything that lay in its path.

He turned to look for the dog, but the dog had gone.

They were within sight of Raoul's house; within sight of warmth and of food — that is if they had anything left, Micky thought suddenly. It had been over a week and maybe the helicopter hadn't made contact yet.

Raoul, coming out of the door, saw the tiny procession of exhausted horses and exhausted men and called to those inside. Within minutes there were hands to help the travellers; Raoul took the stallion and Dick Morris helped Micky into the house. He dropped on the floor, on a mattress that someone had put by the settle, too exhausted to move. Mark and Owen followed him to lie down. Within moments they were all three sound asleep.

Willing hands tended the exhausted horses; they were rubbed and rugged and given hay, and left in the warm stables. The helicopter had made contact the day before; there was fuel for the generator now, and the throbbing was a background to Micky's dreams of pursuing a great dog through the darkness for ever.

The three woke at the end of the day; Micky was aware of hunger — such hunger as he had never known. Sian and Angharad gave them hot soup, and made them wait a while before eating more. Firelight danced on the walls and the refugees sat waiting to hear their story. Gareth's wife knew he was safe and sang softly to herself as she cut bread and buttered it, making sandwiches for the children.

Micky wanted to see the foal; he slipped out, taking a hunk of bread with him and went into the stable. She rubbed against him; the foal was perfect. Everything was perfect; he went to look at Mahruss, and leaned against the big stallion, rubbing his cheek against the soft flesh.

'I think I am jealous,' Raoul said from the darkness.

'No need.'' Micky was jubilant. He had come safely home and he was going to stay here for ever. He planned a future around the stud. He would be headman in a great and famous breeding establishment; they would have the best mares and the best foals in the country. They already had the best stallion.

'What are they all going to do?' Micky asked, as he stood rubbing the foal's ears; she pushed her head against his hand in an ecstasy of delight.

'Angharad is staying with us; and Sian and her husband; Gareth and his wife are having the cottage, so long as he is still policeman here. Their baby will soon be born. Three of the other families are staying. Two are going to relatives, and the Evans' are going to emigrate to Australia to join Dafydd's brother on his farm there. It will be a new world, for all of us, Micky.' Raoul looked out at the morning; a new life was beginning.

Micky knelt beside the foal. She had grown, even while he had been away. She could now control her legs, could buck and jump, and she butted him with her head, wanting attention. The lambs were beside her on the straw, often sharing her milk, though the ewes now were in milk, too.

Micky took her small head between his hands and looked deep into her eyes.

He stroked her neck. The hair grew oddly on either side and he bent to look.

'Have you seen this?' he asked Raoul.

The bearded man knelt beside him.

'Mohammed's thumbprints,' he said softly. 'It is always lucky to have one thumbprint, but this little one has two. It is a sign of great good fortune . . . a sign for the future.'

He looked out at the Old Man.

No one could read the future; not even Angharad, but he knew that this foal marked a turning point for all of them, that she would bring them fortune, though maybe not in the way that they expected.

Angharad stood in the doorway, her blue eyes bright, and he showed her the marks on the foal's neck.

110

'A legend for our children,' she said, smoothing the soft coat. The foal looked up at her and tried to suck her finger.

'Cafell is protecting us; but Rhiannon also has a place to play in history.'

She walked away and looked up at the hillside, where a legendary hound ran for ever, guarding them all from harm.

Raoul led Micky indoors and gave him the certificate of Rhiannon's birth. 'If you stay, she is yours,' Raoul said. 'Your first brood mare. A man needs a stake in life. One day, we will be partners, you and I.'

He looked into a future that was very like Micky's, the horses a passion that they both shared, a link between them, a link that would bond men together wherever horses were bred, in any country in the world.

Everything was the same, whether the mare gave birth on the Russian steppes or in an Arabian desert, in a stable in an English village, or on a Welsh mountain.

Nothing in life was so worthwhile as the tending of horses. They turned together to look at the stallion.

He stood, neck arched, one hoof lifted, posing for them, perfect against the light. Raoul went to him and the stallion relaxed and nibbled the man's ear.

Together they went indoors.

Owen was telling the children the story of their ride; a ride that was to pass into legend, for he had poetry in his tongue. He told of the dark night, the bright stars, and the thin moon riding high; of the glitter on the ground, and the weary men and horses, plodding on for ever. He told them of the dog that came from nowhere and that led them on to safety, avoiding the landslip and the tearing terror of the rising flood, and the sliding death that lay in wait for unwary feet and unwary hooves.

'The Hound of Darkness came to our rescue, and we were safe,' Owen said, ending the story, and drained his beer mug.

Micky reached out for a pasty. He was still hungry.

'Was it Cafell, himself?' asked one of the children.

Owen looked out at the night. Beyond the darkness the Old Man towered above them; beyond the darkness the savage waters flowed where their houses had once stood. Outside in the stable stood the most magnificent horses he had ever seen in his life. Tomorrow he would go back to a farmhouse where he had now trebled his family, and had company, and folk to help with the chores.

Who knew what life had to offer?

'Was it Cafell?' the small voice asked again.

Owen smiled down at her.

'What do you think?' he asked, and the child turned to look out of the window and thought she saw a glimpse of a dog's head, looking in through the lighted window.

When she looked again it had gone, but the wind was moaning softly. High and eerie above the wind howl came the mournful howl of a calling dog; the dogs in the house echoed it, and for a few minutes every noise was drowned by the eerie crying.

Angharad picked up her teacup and looked into the telltale leaves.

'I see a stallion; and a beautiful mare and many foals,' she said.

'What else do you see?' asked the children, crowding around her.

She smiled into the tea leaves.

'I see Cafell, the Hound of Darkness, protecting us always,' she said softly and held the cup so that all could see there, in the tea leaves, the outline of a running dog.

THE END